Destined
TO BE WITH THE
HIGHLANDER

The Lady Of Loch Awe
Book 3

Kalani Madden

KM BOOKS

Contents

Chapter One

Ella saw stars. Tiny white pinpricks of light. They grew bigger, becoming a spectrum of rainbow light pressing all around her.

Now I know what Dorothy traveling to Oz must have felt like. That strange no-man's-land between vertigo and nausea.

She tried kicking out, but it was no use because her final destination was already solidifying around her.

A large, square room lined with pale yellow silk and whitewashed wainscoting. A high pastel painted ceiling, decorated with cherubs, angels, and clouds. Ornately carved gilt chairs with silk embroidered cushion seats.

Wrenching herself free from the magician's grip, Ella stumbled forward, running to look out of the tall sash windows with flattened glass pane squares placed neatly inside the wooden frames. A narrow, cobbled lane passed underneath the window bow leading to a large outer courtyard. As she looked, a man passed by, driving a milch cow before him. The man wore dun-colored culottes with the hem flapping at ankle-length above wooden clog shoes. His jacket was cut short to the waist, and a beige shirt and kerchief finished the ensemble. As if to confirm her suspicions, a carriage rattled past with four black horses, a black coach with yellow wheels, and three liveried servants clinging to the outside of the equipage.

Ella turned back to the man standing in the middle of the room. He was not even looking at her and seemed to have forgotten her existence. He strolled over to the escritoire writing desk at the back of the room and placed his stone inside one of the cubby holes. He took out a key from around his neck and locked the drawer. Only after tucking the fob chain back into his robes did the man turn around.

He had the same sly, crafty expression as the two servants of the stone, Satellius, and Zatlath. Still, his overall look was someone with lofty, intelligent ideals - he had the same eyes as any other smug fanatic.

"Would I be guessing correctly when I say that your family took their eyes off the end goal - to keep the stone safe? Not many people's memories can hold to a promise for five hundred years."

The more Ella looked at the man now, the more his clothing was starting to look like a seventeenth-century silk dressing gown and less like a magician's robe. "Where am I?" Ella knew what a cliché that must sound like, but she was genuinely interested to know.

"A little village called Versailles, Paris, in the year of our Lord, 1673. Do not fear that we will be disturbed by builders - the palace is being constructed one or two miles south of here."

Versailles, 1673. Unbelievable, but nothing that had happened to Ella over the last few months gave her any reason to doubt it.

"Why did you bring me here?" Ella was trying to get her thoughts into a row and believed that question would be a good start.

Making himself comfortable on one of the chairs, the man smirked. "That young man of yours, Callum, and yourself, of course, Mademoiselle Ella Campbell, will never be happy apart from one another. Give us the stone back, and I will arrange for you to reunite."

Ella knew he had a point. Already, she was feeling increasingly agitated, not knowing how Callum was handling the situation back at Stewart Lodge. He had attacked those men! In what way would they retaliate? In such a short space of time, they had gone from being a young couple who were recovering from having their first argument to two people forced apart by space and time once more.

Those niggling doubts that every woman has when her partner is not beside her began to creep into Ella's mind: Callum would forget about her, he would find someone else, how could such a wonderful man feel the same way about her as she did about him?

"Why don't you just wrest the stone from me?" Ella turned away from the window and went to stand in the middle of the room; this was because all the furniture was pushed against the walls, out of the way of anyone crossing the room in the dark.

The man waggled his finger, indicating to Ella that she must bring a chair and sit opposite him. She wondered why he did not call a servant, but then supposed the man probably thought of her as no better than a servant. It was easy sliding the chair across the floor, pulling it behind her: the thick wool rug was as smooth as velvet.

When she was seated, the man spoke: "I call myself the Count de Saint Germain - it is a suitably obscure name, easily mispronounced to sound like a dozen other names of European ancestry. You may call me 'Count'."

"I prefer to call you 'wasting my time'," Ella could not resist interjecting.

The Count made a *tzhck* sound using his tongue and his teeth. "Such a common person with such exaggerated ideas of your worth and station in life."

"Blame it on social media," Ella suggested.

The man rolled his eyes. "Nuts for a parrot. But I must tell you that the charmstones cannot simply be taken. You must give it up, volunteer for someone to take it, or bequeath it to a family member - the stones are very loyal."

That caught Ella's interest. "Was the stone that Black Colin found given up by its previous partner?"

"The one who bonded to your stone fell in love. They gave up the stone to be with the one they loved. The stones do not take kindly to sharing affection."

Ella's brain worked overtime, putting together what Satellius and Zatlath had told her. "Let me get this straight. A magician has to find a stone and bond to it with love. And it is that which enables them to travel up and down the time spiral - but if they fall in love with a human, they must give up the stone."

"Yes," the Count nodded. "It is advisable they do so. One cannot serve two masters, as you know, because it will leave both masters unsatisfied. The first partner of your charmstone cast his stone away - an act of selfishness and defiance. The one you call Black Colin found it. The stone showed its devotion to its new partner by transporting him back to the Lady of Loch Awe…and then Black Col Campbell showed his appreciation to the stone by smashing it into two halves."

Ella cringed at the thought of the hammer and chisel driving down into the heart of the charmstone, but quickly recovered, angry with herself that she was feeling empathy for a magic rock! "Well, he would have cast away the stone sooner or later - there's no way Black Col would choose a stone over his wife. Why do you want the charmstone back?"

"We must have it back because the crystal is extremely precious, outside of its abilities. The elements contained within it come from the land that existed before the ice wall. From whence comes all magick - the place some of you call Atlantis."

Feeling her mouth form into an 'oh' of amazement, Ella did everything she could to suppress it. The realization that someone from the History Channel would probably give their right arm to sit where she was sitting right now made her smile.

"Is that how old you are? All of you?" she wanted to know.

"Time has no meaning to us anymore - nor does age. If I get sick, I move to your era where I can be healed like any other one of your elite. But it is here, at this time, where I feel most comfortable: seventeenth-century Versailles. I can be a noble gentleman and interact with those minds most like my own. Paris is full of doctors and physicians trying to find the Elixir of Life or the Philosopher's Stone. It is really very interesting. Sometimes I jump ahead a few decades, just for a change of scenery, but Paris is where my heart lies, and so therefore, it has become the place my charmstone brings me to with the greatest ease."

"What about going even further ahead?" Ella was intrigued enough to be able to damp down her concerns about what was happening at Stewart Lodge. "Why not travel to the twenty-fifth century? You never know - you might like it."

The Count shook his head. "There is no twenty-fifth century, so I cannot go there. Your time is at the end of the spiral. You have already been told this: Callum Campbell had to wait six hundred years or so for his soul mate to be born. In this regard, the severed stones seem to have been most particular."

After giving this some thought, Ella said in a soft voice. "So, if I had been born during the Victorian era, the charmstone would have found a way to take me back to Callum then."

Shaking his head at her stupidity, the Count smirked. "No, what I'm saying is that out of all the Campbell women who had access to their half of the charmstone, you are the best match. Believe me when I say that not even I understand the mechanism behind a charmstone cut in half, but it makes sense that the two halves would work to become whole again, using the impulse of love to achieve that. And you could hardly expect it to work the other way around; a Highland warrior landing in the twenty-first century might make an excellent plot for one of your silly movies, but it would hardly create a romantic environment for a young couple in which to bond with one another - look at how much trouble twenty-first-century people have falling in love now."

Making a loud scoffing noise, Ella laughed. "Don't be silly - millions of people do it every day! Fall in love, that is."

The Count shook his head firmly. "No. Lust, dependence, habit, comfort, autosuggestion, peer pressure, social pressure, and that broody instinct forcing someone to settle down and start a family - that's all you have. True love is rare, transcendent, and ephemeral. It's an instant attraction without lust. It's kind, helpful, forgiving, and understanding, with no ulterior motive other than to make the beloved person happy.

Ella imagined Callum once more. He was the personification of all those things to her, and he had been so from the start. If that was love, it was a far more subtle emotion than the modern era made it out to be. Ella wondered how she had seemed to Callum when they first met and could not imagine what the warrior had found to love in her. Would he have been the same formidable person if he had come from the twenty-first century?

Callum, with his proud stance and perfectly honed muscles, with his stern, penetrating gaze as he summed up everything around him; a man built and trained for one purpose - to dispatch an enemy in the fastest way. She remembered the adamant way he had told her: *'I am no' interested in the future, Ella, because what if I saw something I wanted to fix or was bound to avenge? I serve my life best in this time and during this age.'*

Although Ella had a strong suspicion that Callum would prove to be just as deadly with a gun as he was with a spear and sword, she knew the twenty-first century would probably tarnish Callum's soul, as it had done with so many others who encountered it. He was a born warrior, but it was so much easier to pull out a gun than to unsheathe a sword; that lazy 'aim and fire' mentality had warped many other normal people's minds that she was glad Callum would never be tempted with it.

She considered handing her half of the stone over to the Count, but she did not want to act foolishly. There was still too much that she did not know, and the warnings of Satellius and Zatlath were fresh in her mind. "Give me a few days to think about your request. If I agree to give you my stone, will you return me to Callum's side, at his time in space?"

"Yes," the man said, but Ella had a hard time convincing herself that he had not smirked as he said the word.

Standing up, the Count moved ahead of her to the door, saying, "I will send a maid to fetch you." And then he was gone.

Ella heard a handbell tinkle a summons, and a few moments later, a maidservant came in and curtsied. "Madame?" She followed the maid out of the salon. They mounted the stairs to a bedchamber on the third floor. Had the Count been expecting her? It was clearly a lady's room. The canopied bed in the middle of the wall, opposite the double glass paned doors that opened onto a balcony, was covered in a blanket of thick satin embroidered with flowers. The bolster was heavily padded with gold thread tassels on either end. As for the canopy itself, its pale gray swathes were fringed with pastel pink and attached to a stucco rose embedded in the ceiling.

"Does the Count live here with family?" Ella asked the maid in French.

"No, Mademoiselle," the maid bobbed a curtsy. "He has others like him visit. That is all."

So, the great mage or wizard, or whatever he wanted to call himself, had other charmstone bearers visit him in his favorite year and place? She wondered how many charmstone travelers were out there. Trying hard not to be too distracted as the maid left to fetch warm water from the kitchens to help Ella bathe in the hip bath in the corner of the room behind an Oriental hand painted screen, she weighed up the pros and cons of giving Count Saint Germain her half of the stone.

Chapter Two

Callum grinned as he stepped in front of Ella so that he might push open the great hall doors for her to walk through. He spoke to her over his shoulder. "Let me amend that glib statement, lass - a Highland warrior feels naked without his plaid an' his sword." Using his thumb, he pointed behind his back, to the sword hilt that rode heavily between his shoulder blades, to make his point.

He looked up to see his father and Laird Gerwain Stewart were not alone as they sat in the middle of the long table on the stone dais in the great hall. In fact, the dais looked very crowded with people Callum did not recognize.

Callum only had to take one look at the strangers, and he knew immediately that the men on the dais with Black Col and Laird Stewart were not from his time or year. They wore foreign garments made from shining cloth in bright colors. The clothes were uniquely cut and sewn as if a hundred tailors had been busy for a hundred years to create such luxury.

Callum noticed at once that the expressions on the wizards' faces were neither malicious nor benign. It was almost as if they were supremely indifferent to the astonishment they were causing. As Callum looked around the great hall, he could see from the widened eyes and open mouths of the servants and Stewart clan in the hall that the sudden appearance of the outlandish visitors had shocked them to the core.

"Your impudence has caused us much discussion, Ella Campbell." One of the men said. He stepped closer to where they stood in front of the doors, walking around the boards and benches in a leisurely fashion. It was after the tall magician in the blue and green embroidered gown spoke that Callum realized the other occupants in the hall were frozen. That was why they looked aghast, stunned with shock; it was because they had been rendered immobile.

"The stone belongs to me," Ella said the words defiantly, but she inched over to stand in front of Callum as if she were preparing for the strangers' reply to be less than friendly. He did not like the way the man in the blue and green gown was moving closer to where he and Ella stood.

Callum drew his sword. It was an effortless decision to make and an even easier action to take. Instinctual.

"Callum, if you love me, don't..." Ella started to turn, her hand raised to stop him, so she had not seen one of the men on the dais moving toward Callum's father, Sir Colin, with a curved dagger in his hand. It twisted him inside to know the men would use their ungodly powers to render someone unable to move and stab them.

It was too late to start asking questions. The young Highland warrior attacked. He was so swift that the magicians standing on the dais opened their mouths to show their perturbation - even the man with the curved dagger stopped in his tracks, cringing back a bit to watch where the young Highlander's sword was aiming to fall.

Suddenly, the man in the blue and green robe moved swiftly to where Ella stood, and the next thing Callum knew, she was gone.

He had never seen such a thing before. No bedtime story his nanny had told him, and no medieval manuscript written by some mad monk raving about how the rapture would tear the holy away from the unholy, could come close to seeing someone actually disappear.

Vaulting over the dais table, Callum wrapped his arm around the man's neck in a tight stranglehold until the poor fellow began making choking sounds. The man dropped the dagger. After kicking the knife across the hall, Callum held the point of this sword out to the three other men, saying, "Divest yerselves of yer weapons, gentlemen. Dinnae think to leave one or two about yer person, else yer friend here-," Callum gave the man who had been carrying a dagger another squeeze with his arm, "might find himself unable to breathe again."

The three remaining men held their hands, palms out, toward Callum. "Our traveling companion was not about to kill your father, Callum. We wanted to cut back his clothes to find his stone, that's all."

"Then remove the curse that renders my clan still and ask me faither to grant ye that boon - don' creep up upon him all unawares. Where's yer honor?"

One of the men took out a charmstone from where it was chained around his neck and drew some symbols on it with the fingertip of his left hand. The people in the hall slowly came awake, rubbing their eyes and yawning. Everyone except Sir Colin. His eyes flew open with instant understanding. Jumping up out of his chair, he drew his sword. "Treason!" Sir Colin shouted.

Dropping his arm from its asphyxiating grip around the man's neck, and then giving him a kick with his foot to send the man stumbling forward off the dais, Callum said, "No, just those thrawn, foutering mages who your Etruscan friend, Zatlath, was warning us about. One of them has taken Ella."

"Aargh!" Sir Colin seemed to snap and rushed at one of the men with his sword raised above his head. Callum pulled his father to a halt, stopping his mad charge with two firm hands. "Let's try honey cakes before we attempt force, Faither. They seem like peaceable fellows."

The four strangers had backed themselves into the corner under the minstrel's gallery. Sheathing his sword with careless ease, Callum bid one of the page boys to guide the onlookers out of the hall, and soon only Gerwain, Callum, and Sir Colin were left.

"Where's Ella?" Callum asked, gesturing to the table and then stepping forward to pour himself a glass of mead. "Where has your friend in the blue gown taken her?"

Speaking faultless medieval Scottish, one of the mages replied. "The one of our order who calls himself Comte de Saint Germain, has returned with Ella to his preferred time and place. He wants the stone. Only when we have both pieces of the charmstone will we be able to use its power again." His collar was still rumpled where Callum had held him in a stranglehold. His garb was as outlandish as his companions: a mishmash of colors and patchwork patterns. The only thing Callum could think to compare it to was a jester at the King's court. He had seen the King's Fool once before, and the way the man was dressed made Callum think he might be a joker.

Sir Colin had obviously told Laird Gerwain everything about the Campbell charmstone, because the laird stood up. "If it's all the same to ye, fine gentlemen, I'll leave. This is none o' my business."

Then it was just the two Campbells left, staring at the four travelers.

"I'll need to speak with Ella afore I decide what to do," Sir Colin said in a reasonable tone. "I cannae just hand the stone over to a stranger."

"I speak for my friends too when I say that would not be possible," the man said, "we can't be sure of the exact whereabouts the Count has taken her."

Sighing as he stretched his arms behind his head, Callum felt the hilt of his sword with a loving, almost sensual gesture. "Och, that's too bad. Do I have to explain to ye what a stalemate is?"

Sir Colin shook his head very slightly, but it was enough for Callum to know he must let his father take over the conversation. "Might I ask where ye gentlemen are from?" Sir Colin asked. "Are ye all together?"

The men smirked. "Nay. We each chose a different time and place to be with our stones," the man with the brightly colored patchwork clothing said. "Mungo," he pointed to one of the men, dressed in bright yellow and green frocked dressing gown with huge leg-o'-mutton sleeves, "Mungo likes to live in England during the Victorian era. Bogdan here; he lives in the land of the Rus, as you can tell from his furs and red silks. Apparently, there is nothing to beat the feeling of galloping across the Steppes on a wild horse during the seventh century, before missionaries and churches were built everywhere. And Tui likes to live on an island, during an earlier era, but definitely, before all you Westerners began paddling around the globe, spreading your diseases everywhere you went."

"And ye, fine fellow?" Sir Colin asked politely. "From whence d'ye hail?"

"I call myself 'Li'l Yo Kay' - I live in the land to the west in your Ella's time, six hundred years ahead of this drudgery you live in now; a country all your monarchs will soon be fighting to lay a claim to, called the United States of America. Being the youngest of them to join the Knights of Khronos, I am very attracted to an art form of rhythmic poetry practiced during the twenty-first century and center my pursuits around it."

"An' do all the Yo Kay clan wear jester's clothes?" Sir Colin wanted to know. "I kent oor spinners an' weavers can make a well spun wool plaid, but how d'ye go huntin' in such garments?"

"I don't hunt for my food," Li'l Yo Kay scoffed. "It gets delivered. Like we said, we each prefer different times and places. What would you say if I take you there and you can see for yourself?"

Sir Colin sighed and stood up. "Well, here's the thing, Sir Yo Kay. I have no desire to be a part o' this anymore. But then again, nor do I want to hand me charmstone over to ye." Turning to Callum, Sir Col gripped his son's shoulder and looked at him keenly, but with a loving eye. "I see what these men mean now when they say they want to belong to a time and a place. But my time is over, Cal. Ye are me dearest blessing an' yer mither, Mariot, was me only true love. Here is the charmstone. Take it. I'm giving it to ye - yer are me son and heir - go with God."

Callum inhaled his breath sharply and bowed his head. "I will do anything to help you bear this burden, Faither."

Reaching up, he took the charmstone Sir Colin was holding out to him, the stone that had once been displayed on Duncan's chest when it was generally believed that Duncan was Sir Colin's heir. All four of the mages gasped, but that was the last sound that Callum heard from them. The great hall, the dais, the men, and his father disappeared.

Callum saw tiny pinpricks of light-like stars all around him. The light particles grew bigger, growing and spreading to become a spectrum rainbow of light pressing against him in a tight tunnel.

And the next thing Callum knew, he was not in Stewart Lodge, Bonawe, Scotland, anymore.

Chapter Three

Ella watched how the maid dressed her in case she ever needed to do it herself, but it was evident soon after the chemise went over her head and tied under her bust that dressing oneself was not ever going to be possible for those fortunate members of the Second Estate.

Before the French revolution cut everyone down to the same size, France was divided up into a three tier class system; The First Estate: the clergy; the Second Estate: the nobility; the Third Estate: the peasants. At the same time Versailles was being built, another more dangerous and more aspirational class of persons was emerging in the towns and villages - the *bourgeoisie*.

Educated, hardworking, thrifty, and disgruntled with the unfair status quo, the middle-class *bourgeoisie* had access to printing presses. After reading a few books and pamphlets about war, famine, and the excesses to be found at court, Paris was starting to simmer with a vague discontent. King Louis the Fourteenth's spectacular ballets would never be regarded with awestruck tolerance again.

The country would boil over into deadly mob rage in only two kings' reigns.

Ella had read Dickens' 'The Tale of Two Cities' often enough for her to know she needed to get back to Loch Awe, just in case the Count decided to skip her one hundred years or so ahead and drop her into the middle of the French Revolution.

Meanwhile, dressing was proving to be a tiresome procedure, and she had to dig deep into her unplugged meditations to get herself through the one and half hours it took to powder her skin and paint her face, and then be sewn into her fine Parisian clothing.

'Unplugged Meditations: How to Nurture the Prehistoric Mindset for True Peace and Happiness' was a book Ella had found online

during her stay at the Waldorf Astoria in Edinburgh. It aimed to teach readers to find solace and serenity when there was no access to modern stimulation: books, devices, and games were all very well, but it was hard to be happy or patient without them. It was rare to see anyone standing in a queue or waiting room without a device in their hands. Therefore, the book was a revelation to Ella, who was facing a lifetime of no bookcases crammed full of Austen, Brontë, and Conan Doyle and definitely no smartphones.

Growing up in Glenorchy had protected her somewhat from outside influences; gaming consoles, pop music, and binge-watching on a streaming service had not been a big part of Ella's life growing up. She had only been exposed to it when staying over at friends' houses in Queenstown, New Zealand, but once her grandmother bought her a phone, the rot had been quick to set in.

Those darn apps had been so addictive. Eventually, Granny Campbell had forbidden Ella to download any app with the dreaded 'in-app purchases' terms and conditions, after finding out that Ella had added her granny's bank card details to her smart device. Ella had been ashamed of herself for surrendering to the lure of ersatz forward momentum promised by the app if she spent a little sum of money in the beginning. It had been a slippery slope from then on, only halting when Granny Campbell had checked her credit statement a few months later. Great Uncle Colin told Ella that the algorithms the apps used to get users to keep spending money were the same kind used in casino slot machines.

"There's no such thing as a free lunch, Ella," Uncle Colin had said wisely. "So it stands to reason there's no such thing as a free app, girly."

One of the Unplugged Meditations chapters was dedicated to helping dieters obsessed with snacking on junk food: an entire chapter devoted to mastering one's hunger pangs by sipping water. Another chapter worked out which emotions belonged to the 'fight' response, which belonged to the 'flight' reflex, and when to listen to them. All in all, it had been a delightfully interesting book for someone facing a medieval future.

Ella practiced the meditation now, allowing her mind to retrieve memories at will, memories that required no camera and no video to recall. Granny Campbell, Great Uncle Colin, all her dear cousins.

As she breathed slowly, their faces came into focus. Ella could smell the dusty bookcases with the tightly packed rows of old books. The storylines of her favorite books came to mind, and Ella smiled as she remembered Granny Campbell telling her about how she had queued at midnight to buy the fifth Harry Potter book before driving all the way back to Glenorchy to read it until the birds started tweeting in the garden.

All their dear faces flashed in front of her closed eyes before fading away as Callum's handsome features drifted into focus, entered her mind, and stubbornly stayed there, refusing to budge.

How she missed him. If one thing could sway Ella into giving up the stone, it was this never-ending cycle of being ripped away from the man she loved.

"Ow!" A pin poked into her stomach.

"*Mille pardons*, Mademoiselle!" the maid gasped. "My hand slipped."

Ella nodded, deciding to leave her unplugged meditations for a while until the image of Callum's face faded from her mind. "*Pas mal, ma chère*, it is not bad. Please continue."

Ella shuffled to the mirror to watch the painstaking process as the maid pinned a white satin stomacher to the sides of her underrobe. The *fille de chambre* - maid - was dressing her in daytime '*habit de cour*', also called a *robe à la française*. It was a spacious, flowing dark orange velvet gown worn over an underdress with modest panniers tied around the waist. The underskirt was adorned with small strass - tiny pieces of cut glass sewn into place with silver thread. The corset had four thick satin ribbons sewn around it and tied to embellish the front.

The *fille de chambre* must have thought Ella's hair was already pale enough because she did not add the powder after coaxing the hair on one side to sit in two long ringlets over her shoulder by wrapping the strands around a hot iron and then spraying the spirals with starch to set them in place. The rest of Ella's hair was pinned up high on her head, with one more white satin ribbon as decoration.

Ella looked at herself in the mirror as the maid dusted rouge on her cheeks in two patches of cherry red. She thought she looked like a doll; one of those porcelain doll's collectors laid across their beds or on tables around the house.

After finding out the maid's name, Ella spoke. "Thank you, Marie," she said in French. "It is very nice."

A bell rang somewhere in the house. Ella looked at Marie, who dutifully informed her. "Le dîner, Mademoiselle."

Dinner. Remembering her thin wrists and scrawny body, Ella asked Marie to show her to the dining room. The chateau was substantial; it took a couple of minutes to get to the elegant double doors that opened into the dining room. Inside contained even more elegance. Seventeenth-century France was definitely not the time or place for her, Ella decided firmly. It was all too opulent and overdone, with the gold paint, stucco ribbon trails, and pale blue silk wall hangings.

The Count de Saint Germain was waiting for her at the head of the table. He did not bother getting up when she entered the room, but Ella could tell that he was not wearing his dressing gown anymore. His wig was a white bouffant surrounding his face, neck, and shoulders; the wide sleeves of his coat and heavily embroidered waistcoat were dark blue satin, embellished with gold thread.

After nodding to the servant who pulled her chair out for her, Ella told the Count. "Knowing the future as you do, are you not ashamed to wallow in wealth in such a fashion?"

The Count snorted. "It has always been thus: what could I do to change it? The second after I try to abolish poverty and outlaw wealth, what makes you think all humans would be content to remain equal to one another? No - the next day, someone would fall into a rage and kill someone, or a group would form to attack and enslave another. Then they would all agree to set up the oldest and wisest to lead them and give them laws. And those old, wise leaders would amass power and money to ensure one of their children took the seat of power after them. Don't be so naive." The Count shoved more food into his mouth, chewing with gusto.

"It's called being hopeful," Ella retorted, but she felt naive saying that, so she changed the subject. "I want to go back to Callum's time and place. How soon can it be arranged?"

She noticed a flicker of emotion on the Count's face. For the first time, the man's imperturbable mask of superiority slipped. He soon recovered when he saw she was waiting for a reply.

"I must wait to hear back from my brethren, the other Knights of Khronos…they are a little late in gathering."

From the slight tenseness in his voice, Ella believed she could take it to mean the Knights were very late in getting back to the Count with the results of what happened at Stewart Lodge. Perhaps Callum's lightning-fast attack had scared them off? "Are you permitted to kill people in your quest for stones?" Ella wanted to know, watching the man's face very carefully in an effort to observe his microexpressions, but the Count kept his face impassive. "Only at the end of the time spiral can we take matters into our own hands in that way - that would be a few days after your mad dash to join the stones together at the museum - because only then would a death not impact the timeline."

Ella wished with all her heart that she could return to Callum and tell him this. She breathed out slowly through her mouth to hide her relief: Callum would be alive and waiting for her at Loch Awe. She was sure of it.

***

Callum stood still, observing the bustling life all around him. There must have been nearly one thousand men building a great white stone structure, as vast as a cathedral without the spire. Some of the men were manning pulleys and others were treading the wheel to lever the stones up to the top of the roof. One of the men noticed him and scurried over to Callum, speaking in French.

"*Écosse*?" The man pointed to Callum's plaid.

"Aye," Callum changed to speaking French, wondering why the stone had brought him there. "*Oui*, I am from Scotland. And this place might be?"

The man looked puzzled but answered Callum politely enough. "You are at Versailles, lad. I put out the word at the ports for more builders. I gather that is why you came here?" The man looked dubiously at the sword hanging behind Callum's back. "How did you get past the guards with that?"

Callum removed the sword from his back and inserted it into his belt to hide it under his plaid, alongside his other weapons. "Och, dinnae fash yerself aboot me sword. I am at yer service, " Callum grinned.

"What is your skill? Woodwork or mosaic? Are you any good at stone cutting?"

He gave the foreman a rueful smile. "I'm starting to wish me family had never gotten into the business of cutting stones at all, *monsieur*..."

The foreman's face brightened. "You cut stone? Good! Report to the scribe with your name. Make sure he writes down the date you start the work. We pay each Saturday so you will not be humiliated when the time comes to pay the church your dues."

"It's not likely that will be a priority," Callum told the foreman in a cheerful tone, thinking about the Bishop of Rutherglen and Father Archibald. Still, he followed the direction the foreman had pointed him in. Callum walked slower, looking at how the white stone blocks had been quarried and laid in place with mortar holding them together. He had never seen such a vast quantity of glass panes before - at Castle Kilchurn, they still used thinly shaved horn, leather drapes, and wooden shutters on most of the embrasures.

As his pathway took him around the palace, the Highlander admired the vast structure in all its glory. Whoever the monarch was who ordered this palace built must have squeezed his subjects for every penny they earned so as to be able to afford it.

Callum knew Ella was close by - he could feel it - just like Zatlath said. It was a warmth, a glow inside his heart. As a warrior, he considered everything that happened to him to be an adventure. He was not at all shocked that a Frenchman would accept his Scottish plaid to be part of whatever timeline the charmstone had dropped him into - Highlanders had been wearing plaid for hundreds of years before Callum was born, so it made sense they would continue wearing it far into the future too.

The scribe was scratching his quill onto parchment on a little makeshift desk in a corner of the courtyard. Despite being seated in the shade, he wore what seemed to be the palace uniform of a knee-length gray-green coat and a small tricorn hat. He looked up as Callum approached him, one eyebrow raised in a questioning arc.

"The foreman put out the word for more workers at the docks. I traveled here in response to it." Callum said calmly, regretting the necessity of the lie. He gave the scribe his name.

"I'm going also to need the name of someone in your family, Monsieur Campbell," the scribe stated firmly, "we lose many men on this wretched building site - the conditions are hazardous, appalling, you realize! I will make sure your money is sent on to them if you should-,"

"Here's the thing, Monsieur," Callum spoke slowly in his deep voice. He was impressed that the Auld Alliance between Scotland and France seemed to be an honest and durable one. "My family is here, but I have misplaced their direction. Do you know of any outsiders living around these parts? He would be almost a hermit with no wife or relations. An aloof-looking fellow, dark of brow and piercing of eye. Small in stature. Possibly rich beyond measure, with no tangible way of explaining it. Living under the name of Saint Germain."

The scribe's eyes lit up. "Ah, Monsieur! Do you mean the Comte? Yes, he lives on the next-door estate. Let me give you the noble gentleman's direction."

Chapter Four

That night, Ella was awoken by Marie. It was not entirely unexpected: the Count had been uncommunicative about why the rest of his order had not been reported to him. Once Sir Colin gave up his stone, Ella's Campbell charmstone would be the only piece left in the puzzle. Ella had gone to sleep with the stone clutched in her hand, wishing for Zatlath or Satellius to come and tell her what to do.

"Mademoiselle. Come. There is one who demands to speak to you."

Finally. The travelers must have returned. Now I will know the best way forward.

Ella's chemise was transparent enough for her to shrug her arms through the lace dressing gown Marie was holding out for her. She noticed her hands were trembling slightly when she tied the ribbon around her waist. Following Marie downstairs, because the maid was holding the lantern aloft so they could both see in the pitch dark, Ella was brought to the kitchen scullery. Perhaps it was the most secretive part of the chateau? But what was the secret?

A man's tall shape loomed in the doorway, with broad shoulders no ordinary French servant could possibly hope to attain without centuries of braw Highlander genetics.

"Callum!" Ella ran forward, flinging herself into his arms. Ignoring the interested gaze of the maid and the night guard, the young couple kissed long and hard. Callum's strong arms held her so tightly Ella felt her feet leave the cold flagstone floors.

"Och, lass," he spoke in fifteenth-century Scots, "I'm no' sure how long it's been, but I've missed ye."

Burying her face into his chest, Ella whispered. "Callum, I will never fight with you again. I have been regretting it so much. Please forgive me." Then, Ella turned to the servants. "This man is my husband. The Count knows him well but disapproves of our union. We will return to my bed chamber."

Ella held her hand out for Marie to give her the lantern. "Do not forget to pinch out the wick, Madame," Marie whispered, bobbing a curtsy. The night watchman grumbled a bit, but Callum said something in rapid French to him and the watchman seemed to accept what he was saying with an understanding nod of the head.

As they walked back upstairs with Callum holding the lantern high above her head, Ella wanted to know what he had said to the watchman.

"Och, I told him we are newly married and wanted to prolong oor beddan." Callum told her with a wink. "I only told him the truth." Ella knew that in the Highlands, a beddan was the equivalent of a honeymoon.

Whispering as they entered her bedchamber, Ella wanted to know, "Who helped you follow me?"

Callum held out Black Col Campbell's heirloom charmstone so that she could see it, saying, "Nay one helped me - Faither said his time was past and handed me this. The next thing I was outside some great palace: Versailles."

"I don't think the Knights truly understand what drives the charmstones, Callum. Don't you agree?"

Sweeping her into his arms, Callum laid Ella on the bed. "I dinnae ken if I could trust any gentleman who chooses to love a charmstone over this-," he loosened the ribbons that held her dressing gown around her waist. The delicate fabric fell open to reveal the diaphanous chemise underneath. Like a hungry wolf, Callum began kissing her neck. It was a sublime connection: his warm mouth tracing the slim arch of her throat.

Feeling ever so slightly ravished, Ella was instantly ecstatic nonetheless. Every time she was with Callum, she fell in love more deeply. Their attraction to one another was still new and fresh. There was no need to force nuance or novelty into the act. Nor was there shame or awkwardness about what tomorrow might bring. They would be together in the morning and every morning after that for as long as they both drew breath.

Falling back from one another, Ella felt the cool breeze blowing in through the double doors that opened onto the balcony. Remembering to blow out the lantern, Ella used the moonlight as a guide and walked onto the balcony after refreshing herself at the washstand in the corner of her room. Her skin was still damp from the water, and she felt the hairs on her arms prickle, but not in such a way that she wanted to put her dressing gown back on.

"What have ye done to yer hair?" Callum asked her, making liberal use of the water in the porcelain bowl on the washstand in the corner.

"It's stuck into ringlets with starch. The *fille de chambre*, Marie, didn't want me to brush it out so I could keep the curls for tomorrow."

Callum made a stifled laughing sound. "Dinnae tell me what year it is, lass. I have no wish to ken. But it seems that women's fashion must always be strange to me."

"This coming from a man whose half-brother wears poulaines so long they look like giant bannock wedges strapped to his toes." Ella reminded him.

They laughed, falling back into bed together after leaving their clothes in a pile on the floor. Touching his forehead to hers as they snuggled closer, Callum murmured. "If I am to guess, sweetheart, I would say the charmstones want us to be unified more than anything else in the world."

"I don't care what the charmstones want, Callum," Ella had to make him understand how blessed, how utterly enraptured she felt whenever she lay in his arms. "I want to be with you for the rest of my life because I love you more than words can say."

He gave a low growl, pulling her closer. "Well then, if you have nay words to help me understand, perhaps ye better show me instead…"

***

The next morning, Callum filled Ella in on what had been said and done after the Count had disappeared with her. They were helping each other dress, just like any other medieval couple in Scotland might have done; Ella folded Callum's plaid for him, and he laced her into her corset stays, chuckling to himself about the discomfort she must feel being trapped inside such a narrow device. Once again, Ella was amazed at how accepting the Highlander was about his new circumstances, but she was fascinated with what he had to tell her as well.

"I can't believe Li'l Yo Kay is a traveling mage," Ella said to Callum when he had finished his story. "The man is a fabulously successful rapper - a type of minstrel poet - in my time; he is virtually unrecognizable without his sunglasses - those are pieces of black glass people put over their eyes to protect them from the sun. But now that I come to think about it, the clothes he was wearing looked suspiciously like a pair of fancy designer pajamas with logos on it."

"Perhaps nighttime clothin' has no' changed that much over the years?" Callum suggested in an offhand manner - he had not noticed what the travelers had been wearing . "So, they decided that night clothes are the most discreet attire to wear as they move from one century to the next?"

"Most people at my time don't wear clothes to bed at all." Ella said as she began pinning her hair up in front of the mirror.

"Noo that's a habit I could come to like verra much during the summer months," Callum told her with one of his most attractive smiles. He gave her one last kiss before they readied themselves to go downstairs.

The morning room was set for breakfast, but there was no sign of the Count. When asked, the servant bowed. "Monsieur le Comte does not leave his bed-chamber until dinner time at noon."

"I guess he must have made an exception for us then," Ella whispered. The breakfast spread of small, sweet rolls, preserves, butter, and hot chocolate made Callum's brows go up. "Where's the porridge?"

Ella poured him a glass of milk after putting half a dozen rolls on a plate and handing it to him. "We must learn to eat when we can, Callum. Who knows when and where we might travel next."

He did not pick up a roll but lifted her hand and inspected it. "Aye, lass, ye're right. Yer bones are as light as a bird, so thin as ye've become. Let's eat."

They ate in silence because they were each deep in thought about what to do next, but also because Ella had the strong suspicion that Callum was one of those men who were not fond of chitter-chatter at the breakfast table. From the way Callum looked around at the gray silk walls and gilt-edged ball and claw spindle leg chairs and then gave a scornful scoff, Ella knew he would not abide seventeenth-century Versailles for much longer.

When they had finished eating, Ella began to tell Callum about something that had been bothering her since the Count had brought her to the chateau. "We are not the first two people to travel to Versailles through space and time."

That caught his attention. "How d'ye ken?"

Turning her teacup around on the saucer with a thoughtful expression on her face, Ella recalled the facts from a book she had read in twenty-first-century Glenorchy. "Because of the Moberly-Jourdain incident, Callum. During the modern era, two elderly ladies visited Versailles and then claimed afterward that they had slipped through a crack in time. They said they found themselves in Versailles, only it must have been about one hundred and forty years before. They saw liveried servants wearing long coats and hats with three corners, and the coats were all the same grayish-green color."

"Aye, that is the color of the liveries the servants wear at Versailles," Callum interjected. "I have seen it with me own eyes."

Pleased to have it confirmed, Ella continued. "But what they remembered the most is how being there made them *feel*. Both ladies said they felt utterly oppressed and fatigued, especially when interacting with anyone because they did not realize they had slipped through the fabric of time. They recounted that everything felt stifling and unnatural, almost as if they were living in two dimensions instead of three."

Ella saw Callum frown. "That means they felt flat and lifeless. So, maybe that's why the Knights have to stay in one specific place - there is only one place where they can feel at home, and everywhere else makes them feel unnatural?"

Callum thought about this for a while in between eating some more bread and butter. Eventually, he came to a conclusion. "Ye have hit upon the truth, I think, Ella. What's the point of long life and great riches if ye feel wretched all the time?"

Marie stuck her head around the door after giving the wood panels a soft scratch. Ella felt much affection for her *fille de chambre* that morning after the maid had left Callum and Ella to dress alone.

"Pardon, Monsieur and Madame, but there are two men asking for you at the kitchen door."

The kitchen scullery entrance was accessible via the herb garden inside the high-walled back courtyard. Secretly hoping it would be Li'l Yo Kay, Ella felt Callum take her hand in his. Should they give up the Campbell charmstones and trust the travelers to return them to Loch Awe?

Ella felt strongly that her love for Callum needed no charmstones in order to exist, but what if she were wrong? If there was the smallest seed of doubt that Callum might grow cold toward her if she no longer held the stone, then Ella was not prepared to risk it. In that regard, love had made her greedy and apprehensive, which was a normal state of anxiety for someone in love to be in as far as Ella was concerned.

They recognized the two men at the door. Satellius and Zatlath.

Thanking the maid and telling the morning room servant to fetch two more cups, the four travelers sat around the small table after the two men had bowed to Callum. "You are the new master of the charmstone. We have never seen such a thing happen before."

"Yes," Satellius said, his face unreadable so that Ella did not know if he was happy or sad about the new developments. "It seems as if the stone no longer needs to be made whole to bring the two of you together."

"When the loop was closed and your father, Sir Colin, passed the charmstone down to you, the two stones joined in one soul," Zatlath suggested.

Callum stayed silent. Philosophizing about the charmstones had never been a favorite pastime of his.

"Which soul?" Ella wanted to know. "Mine or Callum's?"

The two men laughed. "They are one and the same."

Callum swore under his breath before Ella could warn him that their visitors could understand the curses as well as any angry Highlander. "Fouter that nonsense! I want to ken how to return to me castle, and me home!"

"What has happened is new to us," Satellius said, "all we came here to say was this: do not give up the stones! Once the Knights of Khronos have it in their possession, they will command a new facet in the spiral, and they will be able to find the one who cast away the stone for love and punish him."

Ella knew there were worse ways to punish someone other than death - being separated from the one you love came to mind.

"Who cares what happens to some oaf who cast awa' his stone? I cannae blame him if that was his inclination." Callum scowled. "I want to get back home."

The visitors shook their heads in unison. "If you give up the stone, you will be stranded here, you can bet on it. The Bishop of Rutherglen and Sir Colin's second son with Lady Margaret - Duncan

- will have struck a deal with the Knights for you to disappear forever in exchange for the help they rendered."

Callum's brow furrowed as if he had suddenly developed an acute headache. "Are ye tellin' me ye cannae help?"

Ella reached over and stroked his arm. She had never been anyone special in her life or during her time, but it was different for Callum: he was a warrior honed to wield his sword and trained to protect his father's land and his clan: he was necessary. He had a purpose and a pathway leading him in a clear direction. "Don't worry, love," she whispered in his ear, stroking the side of his face with her hand, secretly thrilled from how his beard scruff pricked her fingers. "We'll find a way. Won't we, Mr. Satellius?"

But the two visitors had gone.

Chapter Five

"I don't want the Count to see you here," Ella was panicked now that she knew that the Knights of Khronos had an end game - to find the one who had cast away the stone that Black Colin had found. "Where can I send Marie when I have a message for you?"

Callum shook his head, covering his face with his large hands so that Ella could not see his eyes. It was the most vulnerable she had ever seen him - so helpless at the thought of being stuck at Versailles for the rest of his life. Giving a weary sigh, Callum lifted the charmstone off his neck and laid it on the table in front of him, glaring down at it as if the chain and charmstone were a puzzle he could not solve.

"Let me get this straight," Callum chose his words carefully. "If we give the Count the stones - yers and mine - we are stuck here for better or worse."

Ella nodded. "Yes, and the stones can only be forfeited or passed on; they cannot be taken with force."

Callum cursed again, closing his fist around the charmstone like he wanted to crush the life out of it. "Why does life have to be so complex with these talismans? I thought they were meant to bring good fortune?"

"I guess love is complicated and good fortune at the same time," Ella suggested. "Come, dearest Callum, tell me where I might send Marie to find you later - then you must leave. The Knights don't know where you have disappeared to, which can only be an encouraging thought! I wondered why old Saint Germain looked so concerned yesterday, and now I know. They can't find you - the charmstone has gone rogue!"

"Och, sweetheart, I might as well go and work at the palace seeing as they offered me employment without so much as checking me papers." Callum leaned over to kiss her cheek. "If I sit around, I'll go mad whenever I am reminded of our situation. Let me keep me hands busy with honest labor."

Missing her smartphone like never before, Ella said to him. "If Marie comes with a message, I will give the time we must rendezvous. The only place I can remember at the palace of Versailles is the Hall of Mirrors, so we must always meet there."

Callum gave one of his heart-wrenching grins. "I might ken a wee bit more about palaces then ye do, sweetheart, because I have me doubts that a common laborer would be allowed inside such a fine establishment. What say we meet in the gardens outside the doors of this room full of looking glasses you speak of? Now, let's get that soiled cord off yer charmstone." Removing the old cord from Ella's charmstone's mounting, Callum threaded the heavy silver chain from his stone through the suspension loop of her stone. "Here ye go, that looks less conspicuous. Ye wear the chain, and I will wear the cord."

It took all of her courage for Ella to bid Callum farewell once more, but she was emboldened knowing that he was close by. It had not taken her long to realize that the Count had no idea what was happening. The other Knights were probably searching the timeline, looking aimlessly for signs of Callum Campbell, thinking that it would be relatively easy to hear rumors of a tall, broad-shouldered Highland warrior with a sword hanging behind his back, red hair, and startling blue eyes, in addition to a very combative nature! They would never suspect he was here with her.

After promising Marie that she would gift the maid with the thick silver charmstone chain if she stayed quiet about her husband's late-night visit, Ella was sure that Callum's visit would remain a secret. The maid's romantic nature was thrilled by the tangled love story of star-crossed lovers that Ella told her, and she promised to say nothing about the visit, sensing that if any young woman would be able to change the Count's bachelor ways, it would be Ella.

Marie would tell the night watchman that the visitor had left soon after arriving, and with that, all the loose ends seemed to be neatly tied.

Sure enough, no word of Callum's visit reached the Count's ears. He descended from his boudoir at noon on the dot, simply raising his eyebrow at Ella when she sat down opposite him at the long dining table. "You seem to be in no rush to return to your Scottish lover's arms, Mademoiselle Ella," the Count observed in a lazy, drawling voice.

Touching her neck around which the charmstone hung on a ribbon, Ella hoped the man could not see how reddened her skin was from Callum's rough embrace. "It is a charmstone, Count," Ella said serenely, "not some gewgaw from a bauble stall in the market. Giving such things away takes much debate."

He nodded. "Yes, I understand, and yet you must make a decision soon."

"Please don't tell me that you are running out of time," Ella gave a fake giggle. "Because that's one thing I know you have an abundance of."

The Count tut-tutted. "No. I am running out of patience. At any time, I can give the order for my brethren to make life very difficult for your beloved, you know. Callum and his father would not thank you if they were struck down by a string of strangers popping in to visit out of nowhere. Things like that can be nasty events during the Middle Ages."

With her mouth full of trifle cream, Ella shook her head. "They mot in duh Mimmel Ages - they in duh Memieval Period - big difference."

From the way he rolled his eyes, Ella knew she might have pushed it too far. "If you take me to visit Versailles Palace," she suggested, "it might go a long way to making me feel better about letting go of the stone."

The Count's face brightened. "Why didn't you say so sooner. It would have spared me feeling such antipathy toward you. Let's take a carriage ride over there now.'

Ella shook her head and swallowed her cream. "Mm-muh. No. I want an invite to a proper party. I want to meet the King."

"You want to meet King Louis the Fourteenth, the Sun King of France?" The Count smirked.

"Yes," Ella said blandly. "You don't have to worry that I will tell him you are an imposter - I am not so stupid. And you can introduce me as one of your Scottish cousins - that should wrap it neatly into a bow."

"It shall be as you wish, but if you change your mind afterward, all this-" here the Count gestured to the opulence around them, "-will be gone, and you can spend the rest of your debate time in the cellars."

"Fair enough," Ella said, "but make sure you give me fair warning about the meeting because I want an evening gown - and jewels - to go with it."

The following day, the dresser paid Ella a visit in the evening. After making her a deep bow with one silk stockinged leg and red-heeled shoe pointing forward, the man began to speak. "Ah, Mam'selle is so petite, so demure! There is no question that you must wear white, with maybe a touch of silver. We shall see."

"And Mam'selle's *toilette*?" Marie asked, "What about her hair? Her *maquillage*?"

As Marie and the dresser chattered together in French, Ella tuned them out. The maid had told her an invitation with the Royal seal upon it had arrived at the chateau during the afternoon. The Count had sent word to Ella to prepare herself to attend an assemblée that night. The dresser had arrived with a carriage full of seamstresses to sew the panels onto Ella's undergarments.

Between the two of them, Marie and the dresser, Monsieur Brel, they decided that Ella would be presented to the King of France in a white satin over dress, silver silk under petticoat, and light gray accents of lace around her wrists and neck. Thanking her lucky stars for her unplugged meditations, Ella stood in the middle of the room as the seamstresses began pinning and sewing the outfit onto her body. The corset stays were laced so tightly that her bosom was forced up to become two soft white mounds above the low, square neckline of her gown while her waist narrowed until a large man would have been able to encircle it with his hands.

But even then, they were not finished. Her hair must be curled and lifted into a modish pile on top of her head, and the obligatory two long ringlets must be laid over her right shoulder after a vigorous coating of hair powder had been applied. A jeweled half-circlet was set amidst the pale curls.

The skin of her shoulders and neck had to be dusted with scented talc, and then it was time for her face. This was mercifully quick, as Ella had no smallpox scars to conceal. A light coating of cerise on her face; two patches of pink rouge on her cheeks; a touch of rouge salve on her lips.

Marie stood back to look at her before brushing stray clumps of cerise off Ella's eyelids, and lashes with a brush made out of a rabbit's foot.

"*Voilà*, Mam'selle," she told Ella. "*C'est fini*."

"Finally," Ella let out a short sigh because her corsets were too tight for her to breathe deeply. "Thank you, Monsieur Brel. Thank you,

Marie. Marie, would you please stay behind? I wish to speak with you in private."

When the dresser had packed up the ells of satin and lace and left with his seamstresses, Ella asked Marie to take a pony from the stables and ride to the building works at Versailles. "Ask for my husband, Callum Campbell, and tell him I will be waiting for him in the gardens outside the Hall of Mirrors at midnight."

Patting the silver chain Ella had given her, Marie said, "With pleasure, Madame."

She was impatient to see Callum again but also a bit pleased that he would see her looking so pretty. Even without mascara, Ella liked the way she had been dressed. She looked fragile and ethereal in her white and silver gown. Monsieur Brel had warned her to wait to sit down until she had been handed into the coach. "We need those ribbons and rosettes to stay uncrumpled, Mam'selle, do you not agree?"

Ella did not agree, but then again nor did she want to appear in front of King Louis the Fourteenth with droopy embellishments. The ribbon with the charmstone on it hung from her wrist; just another piece of jewelry added to her. Finding that the best place to wait for the coach was the small balcony outside her bedchamber, Ella waited for the Count to tell her they were leaving, staring at the moon the same way she used to stare at a flat screen television, her thoughts all chaos at the thought of seeing Callum again.

Chapter Six

The Count seemed to have a triumphant air about him as the coach bounced over the cobblestones on its way to Versailles. Ella was sitting next to him so they could both face the front, but she did not like it at all - there was something about the Count when she was forced to look at him close up that made Ella's skin crawl. The skin on his face looked unnaturally thin and tight, so much so that Ella suspected he might have visited a plastic surgeon or two in the twenty-first century. The Count seemed unaware of the revolted glances Ella was darting in his direction; he sat with his eyes closed, leaning this way and that with the sway of the coach, his hands folded neatly in his lap.

Making the excuse that she needed to hold onto the hand strap to prevent herself from crushing her dress, Ella shifted as far away from the magician as possible. He smelt old - musty and stale - as if all the magic in the world was not enough to heal the wear and tear of time. The toll of stretching out life beyond its natural span could be seen in every weary skin pore and hair follicle.

Ella knew she did not want that happening to her, and she wondered if Callum felt the same way.

A trail of coaches could be seen trundling up the avenue, heading toward the Sun King's Court. All traces of building works had been swept away or hidden behind pots of large orange trees. As the coachman brought the carriage to a stop at the wide stone staircase, Ella could hear the murmur of excited voices. A footman handed her down onto the wooden steps, and she was able to look around.

Versailles was huge, monumentally huge. There was no way of guessing the giant structure's mass and dimensions simply by looking at a digital image.

It's at moments like this when I could be sold on the idea of traveling up and down the time spiral, so that I could see what historical buildings of the past looked like. But perhaps I would tire of the novelty quickly...

As the Count descended from the coach behind her and Ella got another close inspection of his feathery-looking skin and the way his bottom eyelids gaped away from the unnatural shining eyeballs, she decided time travel might have a hidden cost she would not be happy to pay.

Holding out his elbow for Ella to place her fingers lightly on the silk sleeve of his coat, the Count said, "Come. You wanted to see the King before you handed the charmstone to me, so here you are. How much longer must I wait?"

Ella wrinkled her nose, her retort limited by her surroundings. "I'm at Versailles, Count. Let me enjoy it without you bothering me about the charmstone for once," she whispered.

Most of the doors on the lower floors were open to visitors. This was done on purpose so that as many people as possible could see the King's wealth. After Ella had gazed on a surfeit of crystal chandeliers, gilt-framed mirrors, and marble pillars topped with wreaths of roses, the Count led her to one of the largest salons.

The room was tightly packed. Everywhere she looked, Ella saw a sea of white wigs, teased, powdered hair, and pale, sloping shoulders rising out of silk gowns. She smiled as she noticed one or two of the courtiers looking up with anxious eyes whenever the sound of a spitting candle could be heard over the general babble of voices. The tallow catchers were wide enough, but Ella would not want to stand under them at the end of the evening.

A hot fug of perfume hung over the room: a mix of rose essence water, exotic middle eastern spices, and sweat. The Count had told her that the King favored Otto of Roses as his particular scent, which sounded strange to Ella, coming from a century where men preferred sandalwood and musk-based perfumes. When Ella saw the long line of people waiting to kiss the King's hand, she decided to settle for catching a glimpse of the monarch and his huge dark wig instead.

"What do you think of our dear King?" the Count wanted to know.

"I think that court artists must be history's version of photoshopping," Ella remarked, "because he looks nothing like his portraits!" After taking one last look at the small boned man with a moon-shaped face seated on the chair on the dais, Ella told the Count she was going to take a stroll around the gardens. "Then we can head back to the chateau. I will rendezvous with you here in the salon." Ella left quickly as another man approached them, obviously eager for the Count de Saint Germain to introduce his pretty protégée to him. She heard the man greeting the Count. "Monsieur, but who is your little friend? She looks so young and charming. Her elegance will rub the gilt off de Montespan's nose if I am not mistaken!"

After peering up at an elaborately decorated clock on a mantel shelf in one of the less busy salons, Ella went outside to wait for Callum. She felt restless and impatient and wondered if this was a physical and mental sign that she was getting tired of this time and place. It was not home - she did not belong here - and no amount of pomp and circumstance would change her opinion.

The shrubbery was cut to less than waist high, probably to deter anyone with plans to surprise his majesty as the King wandered around his garden, sniffing his rose bushes with his little moon face. She recognized Callum's tall outline at once, the moonlight turning the dark red strands of his hair even darker.

She ran the last few yards toward him, and he caught her in his arms to kiss her fiercely. "How is it that I miss ye after only one day, lass?" he murmured, the passion clear in his voice. "And how is it that ye can look so lovely underneath all that white paint?"

Ella gurgled with laughter, hugging him around his waist and rubbing her face against the soft wool of his coat, relishing when she felt the hard muscle of his torso underneath it. "It's cerise - a deadly paste made with lead. I thought I'd give it a try to see what its appeal was."

He shook his head. "Wummin, ye are prettier than the rosy dawn each morn - ye dinnae need such mummery."

"I knew you'd say that," Ella whispered, standing on tiptoe so she might kiss him again. "But that's not what I came here to tell you - I know where the Count keeps his charmstone. I think we should break the lock and steal it. In that way, we'll have a hold over him instead of the other way around. Then we can promise to give the stone back to him after he takes us back to Loch Awe! What do you think?"

"I think we're in the King's gardens under the braw, bright moonlight, Ella. I should take ye in me arms and show ye how much I love ye."

That sounded like an even better idea to her. Callum guided her to where a fountain tinkled melodically into a wide basin. They sat on the edge of the basin wall and fell into each other's arms. It was the most sublimely romantic moment of Ella's life. All thoughts of escape were chased out of her mind as she longed to fall down onto a soft mattress with the man of her dreams.

The sound of high heels tapping on the courtyard paving stones interrupted Ella's boudoir-inclined thoughts.

It was the Count. He gaped when he saw Callum sitting on the edge of the fountain basin with his arm casually draped around Ella's shoulders. She knew then that the other Knights had not said anything to the Count about what had happened back at Stewart Lodge.

"You seem to have become a Knight of Khronos yourself, Callum Campbell," the Count spat out the bitter remark, but Ella knew he was far more flustered than he was letting on from the way his eyes blinked and his hands tightened into fists. "As there is no way you could have slaughtered all four of my brethren, I suggest you tell me how you came here?"

"Why don' ye touch yer own charmstone, Mage? Go find out for yerself what happened, for I will nae waste me breath tellin' ye."

"He can't, Callum." Ella said, watching the Count carefully as she was speaking. "This is his chosen time in space - he can't run the risk of me messing it up for him, because there is no other place where he can feel at home." Ella realized that restless unhappiness would follow anyone who stayed too long in a time where they did not belong, the same as it did with her. It was not that the Knights preferred the eras and areas they had chosen - it was because the agitated feeling was the least frantic there.

The Count shot her a filthy look, but managed to overcome his dislike of this new situation. "I suggest all three of us adjourn back to the chateau. You will be treated with all due respect and housed in luxury. Let us discuss this in my own domain."

Callum stood up, keeping Ella sitting down by giving her shoulder a light squeeze with his hand. Sauntering over to the Count at a leisurely pace, Callum crossed his arms, frowning down at the man. "We ken aboot yer wee secret, Count. The Knights o' Khronos dinnae 'prefer' to stay in the Land of the Rus, or Victorian England, or wherever Li'l Yo Kay lives…ye *have* to live there if ye all want peace. And

Ella is right: we have a lot more bargaining power than ye gave us reason to believe."

Finally, the Count seemed to lose the frigid air of aloof assurance he always seemed to carry around with him. "I bargain with *you*? You are nothing, *nothing* in the bigger scheme of things! If you have been lying to me about the charmstones and what kind of power you wield over it, I swear I will-,"

The Count's right hand moved like lightning toward the pocket on the corresponding side, but Callum was faster. He grabbed the Count's hand before it could dig deep into the pocket. His other hand gripped the mage by the throat. "Och, I really wish ye had nae done that," Callum said, his deep voice hissing through his bared teeth, "because I was looking for an excuse to shake ye like the dog ye are. D'ye think I have forgotten that ye took me, lady, an' disappeared without so much as a 'by yer leave'?"

The Count did not reply. He was making choking noises as his hands scrabbled to loosen Callum's fingers around his throat. A thin 'ack-ach' sound whistled out of the Count's open mouth as his toes tried to find the ground underneath him.

Ella was not exactly enjoying Saint Germain's distress, but she thought he deserved a taste of his own medicine. According to her general knowledge about the last ice age, the Knights of Khronos seemed to have been running things pretty much any way they liked for the last ten thousand years, so it was rather interesting to see the Count's feet swinging an inch above the ground as he croaked out an apology.

But Ella's sense of righteous justice was not to last long.

"Halt! Who dares assault the King's guests?!" Four sentries were pelting down the formal garden pathway toward them, lances pointing at the ready. A few guests and courtiers had come out to the patio, pointing and uttering faint cries as they watched the elderly courtier swinging from Callum's strong stranglehold.

Callum let go of the Count's neckcloth, but the mage did not fall to the ground, gasping and retching. After darting a poisonous look at Callum, he thrust his hand into his pocket again and disappeared.

Chapter Seven

Now it was Ella and Callum's turn to defend themselves, but it was no contest. Callum hugged Ella to his chest after withdrawing the sword out of the inside of his belted plaid, but all the guards did was lower their spears and saunter toward them, tightening the circle of spear points around them.

Callum threw down his sword, and the guards stepped in to tie their hands behind their backs.

A roar of astonished voices could be heard from the Hall of Mirrors. "Le Comte! Le Comte de Saint Germain! They magicked him into thin air!"

As the guards pushed Callum and Ella in front of them, she imagined the expression on King Louis' face when he heard the news. No doubt, the *assemblée* would be brought to an abrupt close as rumors spread.

There would be no more Hall of Mirrors for Ella ever again. The Captain of the King's Guards came riding up to hear the reason for the commotion. He looked skeptical but was prepared to believe the eyewitnesses for now. "Take them to the Bastille. It is there that they shall await judgment at the King's leisure."

They were thrown in the back of a wooden cart and driven out of Versailles. Ella caught sight of an ivy-covered milestone on the side of the road: Paris - 12 Miles.

It was the most uncomfortable journey of Ella's life. She remembered her economy class flight from New Zealand to London with fondness; sitting on the bed of a cart with no hand holds, jolting and juddering along a rutted country lane for hour after hour with her hands tied behind her back - there were no words to express her misery.

Every time she tried to say anything to Callum, one of the soldiers riding alongside the cart would kick his horse to trot closer to the cartwheel so that he might shout at her. "Hey, *mal voisin*! Hey, *chienne*! Shut your mouth." The cerise was making her face prickle, and the pins in her hair dug into the top of her scalp. A blinding stress headache pounded in her temples. As for the corset stays and panniers - Ella had no words to describe the discomfort those garments were forcing her to experience. Her only solace was knowing that the charmstone was still tied to her wrist by the ribbon.

As the sun began to turn the eastern sky gray, Ella thought her despair would never end, but she was wrong. The sun had risen over the hilltops when she saw another milestone: Paris - 4 Miles.

They had been jolting along the lanes since a little past midnight, and they were only halfway to Paris. Ella burst into hot tears of frustration and rage. She longed for the peaceful green fields and lapping waters of Loch Awe.

Callum shifted closer to her, giving her back something soft to lean against so she would not constantly be banging against the cart's sides. The cart driver did not say anything, but one of the horsemen rode closer to make sure they were not talking to one another or passing each other contraband. Ella lent her head against Callum's shoulder, crying quietly until they reached the gates of the Bastille prison at around noon that day. The Paris lanes had been crowded, which delayed their arrival even more as the common folk shouted insults or threw whatever rotten food was at hand.

Ella was thankful for the dinner she had eaten at the Count's chateau because it would give her the strength to go without food for a couple of days, but she felt terrified at what might be waiting for them inside the prison.

"Two prisoners under a *lettre de cachet* from the King directly," one of the guards told the sentry who came out. A few passersby gathered to watch them, but the sentry told the carter to drive them inside and then closed the gates.

"What am I meant to do with him?" the sentry jerked his head in Callum's direction. "The man's family might send someone to look for him - he isn't French."

The guard shrugged. "He's a magician - a great sorcerer - same as her. Throw them into a cell together and feed them through the hole in case they cast a spell on you."

The jailer had bustled over by this time, wiping his mouth with a linen napkin; it was dinner time. "What's all this?"

The guard explained all over again. "The King's guards at the Palace of Versailles saw them make a man vanish into thin air simply by looking at him. There were sundry witnesses from inside the palace too. And he was not just any man - it was the Comte de Saint Germain - that learned nobleman who advises the King in all things. It is a great tragedy."

The jailer gaped. "Well, I never…! Are you being serious? But this is a matter for the church! I certainly do not want them here!" The man made a shooing gesture with his linen napkin.

The guard waved the parchment with which he had been issued in retaliation. "Do your duty. It's not all about eating a nice dinner every day, you know. Their hands are tied behind their backs - untie them once they are safely behind the door when they can no longer cast the evil eye on you. It should be safe enough." The guard edged closer to the jailer, saying under his breath, "Best to give them comfortable lodgings - you never know…" but Ella overheard him and felt a little bit more optimistic about their chances of survival. The Sun King's court could not possibly be a cesspit of superstition and dogma after all.

The jailer slipped one of the sentries a couple of sou and told him to show the prisoners to a suite of rooms in the south tower. Pushing Ella and Callum in front of him, the sentry did as he was told. Ella waited for the man to stick his hands through the hole in the thick wooden door after it shut with a loud thump so that he could untie their hands, but he did not. The sentry's footsteps faded down the passage.

"What do they expect us to do?" Only when Ella spoke out loud did she realize how scared she was; her voice wavered and trembled as it bounced around the stone walls. Callum said nothing. Bending down and laying on his stomach, he craned his neck to look out through the feeding hole. Then he got up by leaning his body against the door and went to look out of the window grate.

"What do you see?" Ella wanted to know, too short to look out of the window herself. Callum did not answer her question. Turning sideways and said to Ella. "Sweetheart, would ye be so kind as to turn yer back to me and slip yer hand under me plaid?"

Ella did not waste time asking any more questions. While Callum crouched down so her hands could reach, and with Ella using her fingers to feel their way blindly up the outside of his leg, she located the leather scabbard hidden under Callum's plaid. Walking her fingers slowly up to the top of the scabbard, Ella found the knife handle and drew it out. "Ye have equal amounts of beauty and wit, lass," Callum grinned as he took the knife out of her hands. He leaned against the wall and began sawing at the rope, holding the knife blade between his finger and thumb. It was a fiddly business, and Callum dropped the knife a few times. He had to lie down to find it again before the sawing could restart.

After what seemed like a very long time, Ella heard him growl and saw the muscles on his shoulders and arms bulge. Callum had finally snapped the cords that bound his wrists. "Come," he beckoned Ella to move closer. A few seconds later, the rope that tied her hands behind her back was falling onto the flagstones.

Ella stayed close to Callum. "What are we to do? That dratted Saint Germain! I wish you had strangled him before he was able to reach his charmstone. What's the bet he has some glib lie to explain what happened, but by then, it might be too late for us."

They looked around the circular room and were happy with the furniture. It must be around the middle of May from the temperature and weather - no reason to have to beg for a fire to be lit in the hearth. As long as the jailer kept them supplied with food and replenished the pitcher of water occasionally, they would not suffer too badly.

Callum would walk to the window every now and again to look at the sun and tell what time he guessed it to be, but soon they realized that all they had to do was wait for the church bells to strike the hour.

"Four on the clock," Ella said in a dull voice. She had not eaten for the entire day now. She was alone with Callum in a lofty tower, but all she could think about was the fact that she had to use the bucket in the corner if she needed to relieve herself.

The door rattled, and the sound of many stamping feet could be heard outside. Straightening her hair as best as possible, Ella joined Callum as they waited to see who was bringing them supper.

It was not two bowls of soup being brought to them on a tray: it was the King. His curiosity about the events had caused him to ride to Paris with his Swiss guard and question them himself.

Four guards ran into the room and held Callum and Ella's hands behind their backs.

Not again. I hope they don't search the room and find Callum's knife. I'm starving and feel wretched. I'll faint if I don't loosen the ribbons on my stays.

But then, all thoughts were driven out of her mind when the King entered the tower room. He was far more magnificent when he was standing up. The heels of his thigh-high riding boots must have been over three inches high. His dark, curled peruke wig was glossy and neat, with curls draped around his face and cheeks to hide some of its wide, pale plumpness. He was dressed for hunting, a raiment which suited him far more than elaborate court dress. One side of his cape was flung over his shoulder to show a dark jacket and sober white cravat. His tricorn hat was held in his hands as if the King wanted to use it as a barrier between them.

Callum bowed, pulling the starstruck Ella down with him. "Majesty, we are most honored. We are humbled by your presence." He spoke flawless French, but it must have sounded archaic to the King's ears. Two hundred years had passed between the time Callum had learned French and the King had been taught by a tutor.

As Ella stood up, she saw a flicker of curiosity cross the King's face. He wiggled his finger to show that the two prisoners could adopt a less rigorous pose, but the guards standing behind them were stiff and ready to pounce if they made the wrong move.

"You speak like someone from one of our more remote provinces, and yet the foreman at our building works at Versailles tells me you came from the docks to work as a stonecutter?"

King Louis the Fourteenth of France ignored Ella as if she were invisible, which made her wish she was.

"Aye, yer Majesty. Me lands are in Scotland."

Callum was playing the game with his cards close to his chest until he knew a bit more about what the King was thinking.

"You are a landed gentleman? How strange," the King waved one leather gloved hand in the air. "It is hard to tell from your clothing - but I hear Scottish wool is very fine."

"Better than anythin' brought from Venice, Majesty." Callum said proudly.

The King waved one languid hand again. "It is not about wool imports that I am here today. I have spoken with Saint Germain."

Ella was so relieved that the Count had returned, she forgot the misery of her tight corsets and headache for one glorious moment, but her elation did not last as the King continued speaking.

"He tells me that ye are both powerful witches and must be burned at the stake."

Chapter Eight

Callum grabbed Ella's arm in a vice-like grip, but she had already let out a squeak of fear. "What is the Comte's story, Majesty?" Callum asked politely as if the King had just told him the time of day and he wanted to prove to Louis that his watch was running slow.

The King looked at them with a neutral expression. Then he leaned to one side as his counselor tugged his sleeve and whispered something into the King's ear.

Ella guessed that Louis was placed firmly between the two chairs of religion and science; she knew the science part of the monarch wanted to have its curiosity satisfied, and the religious side of him was outraged at their audaciousness - practicing magic inside the hallowed grounds of Versailles!

Ella felt horrified that she and Callum were about to fall between the chairs and end up burning at the stake.

"The King will be so gracious as to answer you." The counselor said, "but it is in the interest of his representation as head of the church that he does so."

King Louis the Fourteenth spoke: "I spent an hour or two with the Comte de Saint Germain. He had much to say about what happened. He told me he was desirous of marriage and looked upon the woman as a possible bride. It is because of this that Mademoiselle Campbell was issued an invitation to our *assemblée* last night. The Comte told me that the woman is betrothed to a stonecutter, the man who gave his name to the scribe as one…Callum Campbell." The King seemed to struggle to pronounce the Highlander's name. "And that you followed the Mademoiselle here, to Versailles, hot in her footsteps, so angered as you were by the chance she might choose the Comte over yourself."

Callum said nothing by way of confirmation or denial. His mouth was set into a firm line.

The King paused a bit but then continued when no one interrupted. "The woman left our *assemblée* to wander the gardens. The Comte says he followed his prospective bride only to find her in the stonecutter's embrace. He was enraged, but his strength was no match for young Campbell here, who proceeded to throttle the elderly nobleman's life out of him. When the guards arrived, the young man dropped the poor Comte onto the ground. This can all be confirmed by many witnesses.

"However, this is the part of Saint Germain's story that can only be verified by himself: one demon shot out of your mouth-" here, the King pointed at Callum, "-and another demon came out of the woman's mouth, and the two phantasms enveloped Saint Germain in a fog of invisibility, and then spirited him away, back to Saint Germain chateau."

Both Callum and Ella could see the Count's devilishly clever plot: they were to be burned as witches while he got to continue living his decadently rich lifestyle at Versailles with his charmstone.

"When is the sentence to be carried out?" Ella tried to keep her voice calm, but it trembled all the same. The King ignored her, and she suspected that the monarch might believe that both demons came out of her mouth.

"Majesty," Callum bowed his head as he was speaking. "Grant us one last favor before passin' judgment - please be so gracious as to tell me if the Comte added a request of his own to his suggestion, we be burned at the stake. For example, did he ask if ye might be so kind as to give him leave to collect all our possessions after we are dead? Clothing, jewelry, and anything of that nature. Those who are burned at the stake travel to the site in shriven smocks, not so? The jailer or guards take the clothing in most cases, but I believe the Comte has asked ye if he may take them."

The scientific gleam came back into the King's eye. "Why do you ask? It is a perfectly reasonable request. The woman is wearing some of the Comte's family heirlooms after all."

"I beg your Majesty to return to the Comte and tell him that ye have changed yer mind. Tell him that oor few belongings, and the lady's jewels that are not heirlooms of the Saint Germain family, must be forfeited to the church by way of atonement. The Comte must be purified after comin' into such close contact with demons."

"Why do you ask this of me?" The King asked.

"Majesty," Callum's face was impassive. "I suggest to ye that the Comte will change his mind and his story after ye have proffered yer new decree to him. We are innocent."

Louis gave Callum a calculating stare. A couple of counselors stepped forward on either side of the King to whisper in his ears. The King pinched his finger and thumb together in the air to show he wanted them to shut up.

"We will speak to the Comte again."

And on that gracious note, the King departed, taking his retinue of guards and servants with him.

Ella was close to collapse. No longer caring about whether the mattress was infested with fleas or not, she flung herself down on the bed and burst out into tears of frustration and fear. How deeply she regretted the inconsequential way she had criticized the government during her own time, little understanding of how lucky she was to be able to live her life without fear of deathly punishment or painful reprisals.

Callum came to sit down next to her but quickly stood up again when the bed showed signs of not being used to tall, muscular Highlanders perched on the frames. He leaned over and patted Ella's shoulder. "Dinnae fash yerself, sweetheart. The King is no bampot. He'll weigh the proof before casting an innocent maid into the flames."

Ella found nothing in this statement to make her feel better; it only made her cry louder. Her racking sobs only quietened when the hole hatch at the bottom of the door opened, and this time it really was food.

"While there's life, there's hope. That's what my grandmother always used to tell me." Ella told Callum as she came to sit down at the rickety table, pulling up a stool to be closer to him. This had to be easier for a warrior to bear. Ella decided that because they faced death so often, it could hardly make a difference. She remembered the first time she had seen Callum. He had been cutting brigands into small pieces with his sword, running to take out the man who wielded the crossbow, and casually ducking his head to one side as a crossbow bolt shot past him, missing the side of his head by a fraction. Not only had Callum treated the dispatching of the brigands with ruthless efficiency, but he had seemed equally unconcerned with his own possible death.

Giving a shaky laugh, she wiped the last traces of cerise from her eyes, saying, "Being burned at the stake for witchcraft is considered a repugnant act of cruelty, Callum, but I guess being a warrior has desensitized you to the horrors of mutilation."

He stopped spooning the lukewarm broth into his mouth so that he might look at her amazed. "I'm no' inured to the horrors o' cruelty, lass. What makes ye say that? D'ye think me vicious?"

Pausing her eating, Ella tried to find the right words. She could see she had offended him and thought she might have chosen the wrong words. "Well…you slaughtered all the brigands, and you weren't too upset afterward - by the men who had fallen under your sword or the chance that it could have been you dying instead. In my time, such a thing would have shocked most people."

He did not answer immediately, perhaps struggling to phrase it in a way that her twenty-first brain could understand. When the bowl was empty, Callum pushed back his stool, saying, "The scribe's job is to copy or record words. The farmer's job is to toil in the fields from spring to harvest and then slaughter his kine to keep him in meat for the winter. My job is to guard my faither's borders, kill all those who try to cross it, and accept that I might die in the process. We must all do our jobs."

He was speaking Scots, and Ella translated what he was saying as 'job,' but the literal translation of the words Callum was using was more elaborate: 'that which I am born and trained to do.'

Intrigued, Ella asked. "What was I born and trained to do, Callum?"

He stood up so fast, the stool fell over. Lifting her up so he could hold her close to his chest, Callum whispered the dear words as his mouth traced the arch of her hairline. "I dinnae ken what ye are trained for, sweetheart, but I feel in me heart that you were born to be me wife."

He knew instinctively that it was not the right time and place to make love; he sensed that Ella would be too worried to relax enough for them to join their bodies together and find ecstasy at the end of it, but Callum knew enough to make Ella feel cherished and precious. Holding her in his strong arms, he rocked her against his chest, pressing his mouth against the top of her head so that she could feel how even his warm breathing was. Ella found it impossible for her to panic when the steady beat of Callum's heart was soothing her anxiety.

After rinsing out her mouth with water from the pitcher - Ella was still watching her liquid intake because of that bucket in the room recess that she would be forced to use as a toilet - she allowed Callum to lead her over to the bed. The sun must have been sinking in the horizon because the shadows in the tower prison were lengthening.

"Maybe we should hide our charmstones in here," Ella suggested as they lay down on the bed together, ignoring the ominous creaking that came from its frame. "If I die, I would not want the Count to have mine - I don't think the charmstone would be happy with that."

She felt laughter rumble in his chest. "Och, Ella Campbell, ye're like a dog with a bone that ye won' stop gnawin'." Callum shifted to his side and took Black Col's half of the charmstone out of his pocket. He held it up above them, turning the talisman this way and that as the crystal caught the last rays of the setting sun and reflected it back at them. Ella was inspired to remove her own charmstone from her wrist and hold it above them as well.

"Such a story these rocks might tell," Callum murmured as the two crystals twinkled happily together. "But I would cast mine away in a second if I was forced to choose between ye or it."

Ella turned to tell Callum that she would do the same, but he looked so handsome lying next to her that she changed her mind and kissed him instead. "I love you more than anything, Callum, and I would follow you to the end of the world if it meant us being together."

And just like that, the prison cell disappeared as their two charmstones were brought together.

Chapter Nine

Callum and Ella found themselves underwater, but did not panic. Callum was a fighter, always prepared for others to try and take him unawares; Ella had this happen to her twice before. Clutching at Callum's arm, she allowed the air in her lungs to float her to the top.

They emerged, spluttering and blowing, holding onto one another and their charmstones. Callum did not need Ella to tell him that they were at the spot where they had first met. He knew every rock and tree inside his father's domain.

Ella was finding it difficult to stay on the surface. The panniers and heavy fabrics of her dress robe kept dragging her down. Without her having to say anything, Callum slipped one arm around her chest and began to kick backwards toward the shore. After hauling her onto the sand and pebbles that made up this part of the coastline, Callum withdrew the knife he kept hidden under his plaid.

"Is it our time?" Ella said, in between panting and gasping. "Try and find a sign."

After glancing back at her to make sure Ella would be able to crawl further inland on her own, Callum waded to the rocky outcrop that was blocking their view of the other side. He climbed the wet stones and, looking over the crest, shouted back to Ella. "Aye, lass. There's the cairn where I tied that wispy garment o' yers to the spear. No' much has changed."

Ella did not have much religious conviction, especially after meeting people like Father Archibald, who positively licked his lips at the thought of seeing her naked, tortured body. Still, she fell to her knees after hearing Callum's words, whispering fervent prayers of thanks. She wanted to be done with traveling forever.

Callum did not join her but clambered over to the other side of the rocks, balancing with ease on the smooth, slippery surface. He waded to the shore where the mound of stones formed the cairn. The sun must be rising on a new day because the eastern skies were lighter than the rest. The air was chilly but not frigid. The Highlander judged the season to be May, the same as it had been when they had been forced to leave. As Ella dragged herself around the rocky outcrop to join him at the cairn, holding the heavy panels of dripping wet dress robes in her hands, Callum shouted over to her. "We must travel to Stewart Lodge to retrieve yer belongings, lass. Are ye up for it?"

Amazingly, Ella could still feel broth from the seventeenth century sloshing around inside her tummy. "Yes, indeed I am. I just need to remove some of these darn robes." Standing on the beach, Ella began to pull the pins out of her hair. Thick globs of starch clumped the strands together. Revolted, Ella raised her voice to call Callum. "Please help me unlace this robe! I have to wash my hair in the water. I won't be seen like this."

"Och, lass, ye are comely enough without worriting aboot yer hair." But he helped Ella untie her stays. "Just cut them off," she said, itching to wade into the water and sink beneath the waves.

"Nay," Callum said firmly. "These fallals must be worth a small fortune once they are dry. With the Bishop of Rutherglen soon to be breathing doon oor necks, we'll need to find a way to sweeten the King's mind toward us - these precious stones and fine lace might be just the thing to do that."

Leaving him to spread her French finery on the rocks to dry and giving him her half of the charmstone to hold, Ella ran back into the water to wash the last traces of seventeenth-century France out of her hair. As she bobbed amidst the waves, she thought about what Callum had said: they were back in medieval Scotland, which meant the men who had sworn allegiance to the Knights of Khronos would be after them. She hoped King Louis the Fourteenth had taken the Comte de Saint Germain to the dungeons to be interrogated or at least inconvenienced him with many questions about why the man might have lied about being spirited away by demons.

So long as he has something else to think about besides us, we should be all right. The Count would do anything to keep his time in space safe and secure.

After watching Callum hanging her under petticoats and chemise dress from the branches of a tree, Ella spent the rest of her bathing time thinking about how to make the outfit appear medieval. Emerging from the water sometime later, her hair finally free of starch, Ella shivered. There was no towel and no sign of Callum. Treading up to the tree line, her feet aching as the pebbles ground underneath them, she looked east for an indication that it was going to be a sunny day.

But they were back in Scotland, and once again, the pale yellow sun rose a few degrees into the sky before going to hide under a bank of gray clouds. All Ella could do was pray it did not start raining; as she watched, the clouds seemed to grow darker, amassing into ponderous carriers of thunder and drizzle.

A snap in the trees made her startle.

"Hoots, Ella, ye're jumpy as a cat." It was Callum. Throwing the pile of dry wood he was carrying onto the sand and pebbles, he pulled moss kindling out of the pouch hanging from his belt and began lighting a fire.

"The rain is coming, I think." Ella tried hard not to sound like a jumpy cat.

Callum shot a look up at the clouds. "We have an hour or two." The fire grew larger, and so did Ella's optimism. The thinner cotton and silk garments hanging from the branches were swaying in the breeze out of reach of the flames, but they would dry quicker now that there was heat. Ella watched enviously as Callum sat down on the ground to untie his boots, which were now possibly the dampest part of his clothing. She knew from her modern life that woolen clothing repelled water and was the recommended material for most expeditions and outdoor activities - most of Callum's clothes were waterproof: his wool plaid and his flax linen shirt. Only his leather boots would need to dry by the fire.

The fresh sea air was invigorating despite the early hour of the morning. Callum was not at all worried without the ringing of the chapel bells to let him know what hour was on the clock; all he had to do was look up at the sun's position in the sky. "It's early," he told her, "nigh on six or seven bells after the midnight candle has guttered in its tallow catch."

She watched him unpin the great kilt from his shoulder as Callum allowed the garment to drop down behind his knees. Shrugging out of his shirt, he handed it to Ella. The garment was damp and smelt of smoke, but it was heavenly compared to standing close to the fire, shivering and naked. Once again, Ella was amazed at how closely their minds were aligned without the need for communication. It was as if he felt her discomforts and moods without her telling him.

"What else do you have hidden under that plaid of yours, Callum?" she smiled, sitting next to him beside the fire, tilting her head with a teasing look on her face. His chest was still slightly damp and glints of sunlight cast his muscles into shadow. Elle could look at him all day and never get tired. "How many swords?"

He shook his head, but she could tell Callum was sad. "Those fouterin' Swiss guards of the King's took me sword. 'Tis a shame, but not enough to make me want to go back there and fetch it."

Lifting the side hem of the plaid wrapped around his waist, he showed Ella how leather handles were sewn onto the belt and then hidden inside the waistband. "Then I tie the sheath to the handle, and it hangs under the plaid. But I think that the French King knew I had weapons - and he also knew I would no' use them on him. He's a canny one, auld Louis. He suspected the truth the moment the Count started spouting nonsense aboot demons. Too bad oor escape will cast doubts on us again."

Ella shuddered. "Don't remind me of that - the dastard mage wanted us to be burned at the stake!"

They sat next to the fire, comparing memories of their time in France and what might the Knights of Khronos try to do next.

"I touched the charmstones together when ye were dunking yer hair in the water, sweetheart," Callum told her in a careless manner.

She gasped. "What?! You might have disappeared to some unknown part of the world, Callum! Whatever were you thinking?"

He shook his head, staring at the flames in a distracted manner. "Nay, ye are wrong. This is oor time an' oor land, and everyone we care aboot is here. Why would the stones want to move us away from it?"

There is still so much we don't know about the Campbell charmstones. After all, they are the only cut stones in existence; they might march to the beat of a different drum.

Ella's hair dried, and after a while, the petticoats and underskirts began to float in the wind as the fabric lightened. After getting up to touch it, Ella told Callum they could break camp and begin the long walk to Stewart Lodge all over again. "Let's go and set your father's mind at ease," she said, "it must have been at least four days since our disappearance."

Pulling the chemise over her head and tying two of the petticoats and a silk underskirt around her waist, Ella was ready. She had given the shirt back to Callum, and they acted as one another's mirrors to make sure they looked presentable. Even though the dress, robe, and stays were still damp, Callum bundled them up and tied the garments over his shoulder. He placed the jewelry in a pouch.

Thunder rumbled above them as they walked along the coastline. Ella looked up anxiously, but Callum fixed his eyes on the inlet waters lapping at the shore. He was checking the tide and rate the waters were sweeping into the loch. When the rain finally set in, he told Ella it was mid-morning and that they had been walking for three bell tolls while wrapping a portion of his great kilt over her head. It kept the rain out, but that was small comfort to Ella, who was sick of being wet. She grumbled that she missed her digital watch, and the rest of the hike was spent talking about medieval timekeeping, with Callum insisting that burning candles and ringing bells was the best way to tell the passage of time from one half of the day to the next.

When they reached the Lodge's gatehouse, Ella's stomach told her it was dinner time. She knew enough about medieval life to know that a small breakfast was eaten at dawn and the main meal - dinner - was eaten at around noon. A bowl of soup was supper before the candles were snuffed out, and the whole process started over again the next day. When she told Callum that it must be about noon, he looked up and the storm clouds overhead and told her it was closer to the middle of the afternoon.

"I give up," Ella huffed. "I'll never get fifteenth-century time-keeping correct."

The gatekeepers looked at them with puzzled expressions. "Good morrow, Cal and Lady Campbell. Did ye venture out for an early morning walk?"

Callum scoffed. "Nay! Are ye raving? The rain was so thick it could have filled a vessel in the blink of an eye!"

The gatekeepers shook their heads as if they thought he was joking but let the young couple in without any more chat. "Belike they are all still at dinner. Go on to the great hall."

It seemed as if life at Stewart Lodge was carrying on as usual. "Me Faither must have kept his mouth closed about what happened in the hall after we were removed." Ella shook her head. "How strange that there is not more of an uproar about what happened. I would expect the priest to be called at the very least."

They entered the great hall, and Laird Stewart hailed them with good humor. "Och, where have ye two lovebirds been a-dallying? Come and break yer fast! We have nae seen hide nor hair o' ye since this morn."

Immediately, Black Colin got up from his chair and scurried over to them. When he reached them, he pretended to embrace his son, but giving Callum a hug was not all he was there to do.

"Say naught about what happened. The laird's memory is foggy about those outlandish visitors - and as for the rest o' them, they cannae remember a thing!"

Chapter Ten

"What are ye saying, Faither?" Callum whispered, all the while pretending to return Sir Colin's embrace. "What time is it?"

"As far as Laird Stewart is concerned, the two o' ye dinnae even come to the hall for breakfast! He's been cracking jests aboot yer bedchamber cavortin' keepin' ye a-bed all morning. 'Tis dinner time noo. Ye have been gone all morning."

So, the mages had appeared at the breakfast table, but the crystals had wiped the clan's memories free of it. Callum and Ella had been brought back to the same place and at the same time, bar some traveling to the Lodge.

Sir Colin shot a look at their clothes. "Ye look unruly. What excuse will ye give?"

Callum gave his father a wink and stepped closer to the dais. "A fine day I thought it was for wanderin' the bonny Bonawe hills, Laird! Little did I guess oor venture would end in such damp disarray. Please be so kind as to give us leave to retire to the chambers to change?"

Much laughter and pointing of fingers accompanied this statement. "Och, awa' wi' ye!" Laird Stewart shouted, holding his sides he was laughing so uproariously. "An' never call yerself a Highlander again, Cal! No' until we have forgot this wet wanderin' o' yers!"

They backed out of the great hall as fast as they could. Ella noticed some ladies in the hall pointing at her petticoats and underskirt and whispering behind their hands. It was possible that silk that was so fine and well-made had not reached the Highlands yet. Not bothering to take them off when she got back to the bedchamber, Ella pulled a wool tunic from her backpack and pulled it over her head. After the tunic hem had fallen down to her poulaine-shod feet, she was a medieval maid once again.

"Don' forget to hide yer hair, sweetheart," Callum said to her as he inspected his beard in the looking glass. "'Tis too pretty to be left on show for every man's eyes to see an' admire."

It warmed Ella's heart to know that she was back in a time when men could find a woman's hair so alluring that she must keep its arousing properties hidden from view. A ripping sound caused her to turn around, and she saw Callum had torn one of the ribbons from her court dress in half, and he was busy threading the thin silk cords through the loops in the charmstone's settings. Without saying anything, he handed Ella her charmstone, but when she reached out to take it, he grabbed her hand and kissed it - yet another one of their silently intimate communications. She noticed the small furrow that had marred his brow when he was in France had gone, and she wondered how displaced Callum had felt when he had been torn away from his place in time.

He is so brave and uncomplaining. It makes me feel petty and mean-spirited for grumbling so much. I must try to leave my twenty-first-century ways behind me. They are no use to me here.

When they returned to the great hall, aside from a few more jests about Callum going out for a walk in the rain, their tardiness seemed to have been forgotten. Ella was seated on Callum's right, and he was next to Sir Colin. They whispered amongst themselves as much as they could without appearing too rude.

Just like his son, Black Colin was disinterested in hearing about anything outside his realm of reality. "It is imperative ye hang onto those charmstones o' yers." Sir Colin insisted on telling them. "I have never seen such a wonderful thing in all me life before, Cal! One moment ye were here, an' the next - gone!"

"So, no more letting the talisman sit in me mither's tomb then?" Callum asked with one raised eyebrow. Sir Colin shrugged his shoulders. "I care not. My time with the stone is over and I am much relieved about that. But I still do not relish Maid Ella's craven ancestors makin' off with it." He scowled in Ella's direction, so much so that she felt ashamed of being descended from the Bishop of Rutherglen as if he was her grandfather, and not some ancient, distant relative.

"Hush, leave Ella alone. She has no power to change things now, nor would I have it done so. But I wish to return to Kilchurn Castle as soon as we may. I foresee a siege at the very least."

Ella did not like the sound of this at all, but Sir Colin was holding up one finger toward them for silence and clearing his throat. "Oor foster daughter - yer daughter, young Margaret, who is now one o' me wife's companions; who will ye have her betrothed to, Laird Gerwain?"

Pausing with a spoon halfway to his mouth, Laird Gerwain Stewart considered the question. "Och aye, she's at an age now where her husband will want to take wee Margaret under his wing an' keep watch over her until she is auld enough to breed…what d'ye say to her joining with Duncan? He might no' be yer heir anymore, Col, but he's yer blood. Margaret's mither was a fine, strapping wummin. Belike they will make a fine match of it?"

Sir Colin seemed to give the matter some thought before he replied. "Nay, auld friend. Let the girl stay bonded to Bishop Rutherglen's nephew, Glynnis. I'm at odds with Duncan an' Lady Margaret over this matter," he waved his hand at Ella and Callum sitting on his right. "But I do not wish to tamper too much with what has already been decided in case it changes events in the future."

"I could not agree more," Ella said, "I think we should leave things as they stand when it comes to the Bishop's kin - they are my ancestors when all is said and done!"

Sir Colin ran his hands through his thatch of graying hair. "Losh! I had forgotten. We would be in a vinegar pickle if those who came afore ye were to change, Ella!"

The two old men nodded at each other, indicating they would talk further in private.

Callum said nothing, but Ella could tell he was thinking. No, thinking was the wrong word: Callum was strategizing. When Sir Colin left the hall to discuss Margaret's betrothal, she asked Callum about his plan.

"So, ye noticed I had a wee bit on me mind, did ye? I was thinkin' that we need to get off this watery isolation surrounding us, sweetheart: we must go home."

Callum marched out of the great hall, looking for Steward Martyn. Finding the man wiping his mouth after a trip to the wine caskets in the cellar, the Highlander cornered the steward, who looked guilty. Callum reassured him. "Hoots, I dinnae care if ye've been takin' a wee sup from the fine wines, fellow," he told Martyn, who immediately lost his guilty demeanor and asked Callum what he could do to help him. "I need a boat with six rowers to take us upriver to Kilchurn."

Full of good humor, the steward bustled off to command them a boat, of which there were many because the lodge was surrounded by water. Callum left word with the manservant. "Relay this message to me faither, Sir Col: tell him that we have gone on ahead to tally those men still loyal to us."

The servant bowed and then went to help the page boys carry Ella's backpack and the bundle of French court dress to the boat. They sat in the bow, away from the rowers who might be able to overhear them.

"Won't Laird Gerwain be offended that we left without saying farewell to him?" Ella worried.

Callum gave her a quizzical look. "Nay, he's more likely to be offended if we were to stay there hiding an' pretending that we were no' facing an insurrection."

"What insurrection?" Ella wanted to know.

Calmly, as if he was talking about what he hoped would be served for supper that evening, Callum explained to Ella. "When me faither handed me the charmstone, he handed the control of his land and fortune to me as well. He has forfeited all of his influence. I might ask him for advice or choose to heed his wise counsel, but from here on, every step or misstep I make is mine an' mine alone. Thus, we will find certain clan members, such as Duncan, Father Archibald, and the rest, reluctant to accept this. They will revolt - that is an insurgency. "

He saw Ella open her mouth to say something but cut her off. "Aye, I ken what ye said to me aboot us being equals an' that I must no' make a decision without ye, but this will be a battle - an' ye will have nay part of it, dear lass."

Ella moved to hug him, but Callum flinched back - he had not finished talking. "An' I dinnae care how much ye smite me around the heid, Ella, I'll no' cry ye mercy. Ye're no' to involve yerself with the fightin' an' that's me final word on the matter."

She smiled, "I wasn't going to 'smite' you; I was going to embrace you, but I'm pleased you listened so carefully to my complaint after our previous brangle." Ella adored it when Callum used words she associated with the King James Bible or any other ancient text. It was at moments like that when she felt a true thrill that only life during the Medieval period of the British Isles could give her.

They laughed softly together. Their fight seemed so long ago. Had it been two hundred years ago or two days? It was sometimes hard to tell.

Rain was still in the air, and the clouds above them were heavy with it, but as the rowers pulled them up the River Awe, closer to Castle Kilchurn, the young couple grew more hopeful and peaceful as the riverbank slid past. A goshawk - perhaps the same one that had circled above them on their first trip upriver together - wafted on its wings high in the cloudy gray sky, giving a plaintive cry. The soft dreich drenched the land, softening the rich, black soil and wetting the cragged rocks.

Ella closed her eyes and lifted her face up. The dreich clung to her skin, forming dewdrops that glistened and bulged before falling down her cheeks like tears. For some reason, Ella found the sensation unsettling. When had she last cried that hard?

When her dog, Gillespie, died. He was a shaggy rescue mutt whom Granny had allowed Ella to choose for herself on a visit to the shelter. The little shaggy white dog was nothing special to look at, but the sparkle in his loving eyes had spoken to her louder than any words. Gillespie had never fully recovered from the neglect and abuse he experienced as a puppy, from the scars of chain marks around his neck to the missing teeth from where he had tried to gnaw himself free, but his spirit was resilient. But having a fighting spirit was not enough; Ella and Gillespie only got to live together for six years.

The memory of her poor little dog eventually submitting to the diseases that ravaged his frail body had the power to make Ella shut her eyes tight and make her throat close in a hiccup of misery. With all this skipping around from era to era, she had forgotten how fragile life truly was. And now they were rowing toward war. Callum could call it an insurgence as much as he liked, but Ella was ready to rip her figurative blindfold off. This was a place in time when women were treated like empty vessels, and men walked around with swords hanging behind their backs just in case they were attacked.

When she opened her eyes, Ella noticed Callum looking at her with concern. Maybe he was thinking about the same thing: witch burning and rape and death, things that Ella was most definitely not trained to deal with.

"When we find a fair-minded priest, Ella, we must be wed. How d'ye like the sound of becoming the Lady of Loch Awe?"

It was the last thing Callum said to her. As the boat rowed closer to the riverbank, a rustle in the reeds was the only warning they had to alert them that a man with a crossbow was hiding there. A heavy thud was heard as the quarrel bolt shot out of the stock groove, and the trigger was pulled. Callum grunted as the bolt embedded in his chest, spinning him sideways as he fell back into the boat.

Chapter Eleven

Time stood still. Shock and horror froze Ella for one split second. Then the first aid courses she had attended in Edinburgh kicked in.

"You, drop your oar and fetch that sack."

The rowers were heaving at the oars as if their lives depended on it, but Ella was fairly sure the crossbowman had been a lone assassin, not an army. Fortunately, Callum had fallen sideways into the boat hull, which gave Ella the perfect opportunity to check the wound without having to lift him. The quarrel bolt had gone straight through the upper right area of his chest: the tip was protruding out of his back in the middle of the shoulder blade, a thin wooden fletching stuck out in front. Callum was stunned, panting, in shock and great pain. Ella crouched next to him, rubbing her hand up and down his arm in a soothing gesture, her lips pressed together to stifle her screams.

Two of the rowers crawled over to Ella, hauling the backpack. Of course, if one oarsman was helping her, the other one would not be able to row. "Go and keep lookout in the bow," Ella ordered the spare rower. Turning to the other, she said, "Open that sack and start taking out that which you find inside it." The man dutifully began removing items of clothing and small pouches of valuables until reaching the packets of medicine and first aid kit that Ella had packed into waterproof plastic bags at the bottom; the man hunkered as low as he could without actually lying down in the hull, his eyes darting from one side of the river to the other as he watched for other attackers.

While he did this, Ella began administering to Callum's immediate needs: checking his pulse and breathing, and seeing how much blood he was losing. Both wounds were oozing dark blood, but there was no gushing. She knew this meant that most of the blood loss would be occurring inside Callum's chest cavity if one of the main veins or arteries had been nicked.

The blood is dark, and the bolt went through on the right side of the chest, which means the red blood holding all the oxygen is still viable. Out loud, Ella said, "Stop! Open that…packet. Take out the parchment inside." It was an anatomical drawing showing where the bones, muscles, nerves, and blood vessels lay in the body.

Using her fingers to measure, Ella worked out the bones and muscles that might have been damaged. It was difficult - Callum had bigger muscles than any anatomical drawing could ever hope to represent. Then it was time to check if any veins and arteries might have been hit, but from looking at the bolt angle, Ella felt optimistic about her lover's chances.

Callum groaned as she pulled him from leaning forward and then back again, pressing her fingers between his shoulder girdle bones and spine. The riverbank was elevated, higher than the loch water, which meant the quarrel bolt had entered high and exited low, pinning him under the clavicle with the point smashing out of his scapula. Trembling but determined to be brave, Ella decided to leave the bolt in Callum's chest. The quarrel had penetrated in a downward trajectory, lodging itself under the collar bone, deep in the upper pectoralis muscle.

After pressing her ear to his chest and listening to his breathing, Ella was positive the lung cavity was still working normally: Callum's short gasps were from distress and not because he could not breathe. When she moved Callum to see which bones and muscles had been perforated in his back, he went from shock to unconsciousness, slumping heavily into the bottom of the boat, leaving Ella alone in his medieval world.

Ella calmly checked the quarrel tip sticking out of Callum's back muscle and then left him slumped in the boat after making sure the bolt was not touching any surface. "You two men - move the Laird's foster son, so the boat stays at an even keel and then return to rowing. We must make haste to the castle."

"Ye dinnae have to tell us that twice, hen," one of the rowers muttered under his breath, and indeed, the boat was slicing across the water at a breathtaking speed. Ella sat forward in the bow, looking out for any person lurking in the thick bushes on the water's edge, but they had already reached the loch, and the oarsmen made sure to keep the boat out of the line of fire from a crossbow. Longbows, however, were another matter entirely. Ella gnawed her fingernails to the quick as she scanned the shores.

"Ye cannae hide a longbow amidst these short bushes, lady," one of the rowers told her, "that much Auld Black Col took care of - he kept the foliage pruned back."

"The man is no' so much a 'Black Col' anymore as he is a 'Gray Col,' lad," another rower quipped. "Mayhap the auld fellow will join his wife in her crypt soon enough."

Ella was amazed that Sir Colin's death would be a topic of conversation. The Knight could not be much more than sixty-five years old. But then she realized they were living in an age where there was no medicine other than what could be brewed in a kitchen, and changed her mind about what the definition of old age might be.

The men slowed down their furious pace as Kilchurn Castle hove into view. Ella thought it was the best time to administer an injection. Riffling through the backpack until she found her syringes and pristine clean little bottles of medicine, Ella gave Callum an injection of antibiotics and something for pain relief into the hard muscle of his right bicep. She judged his weight as close to one hundred and ten kilograms or so, but Ella was not sure. What with this being her first relationship and herself not being the sort of person to worry about her weight, she had no clear idea about what a well-muscled man several inches over six feet tall should weigh, but he was clearly nearly twice her size and bulk.

I don't suppose giving a bit more pain meds will matter that much once we start trying to pull out that quarrel bolt...

The makeshift builders' huts were still on the hillside, out of reach of the spring equinox tides. One of the rowers blew a horn, and immediately Ella could see heads popping out of embrasures in the castle tower walls and children running out of doors. By the time the boat drew close to the jetty, there must have been dozens of caring hands to help lift Callum carefully out of the boat. Ella asked one of the builder's children to carry her backpack after she had checked to make sure the emergency first aid medical was in her hands.

"Take Captain Callum to his bed-chamber," Ella requested after she saw them heading for the kitchen.

"But Milady, the kitchen has hot water and herbs and a table. We can always carry the captain to his bed-chamber after the bolt has been cut out."

Bowing to their better understanding of where to treat a wound, Ella allowed the men to place Callum onto a stretcher made of leather hides, cord rope, and branches and heave him up the narrow castle steps. It was perilous, tramping up the high stairs with no balustrade to hold onto, and Ella clutched the first aid pack to her chest as if it were a priceless treasure.

At least once we are inside the castle, we will be safe from attack. That reminded Ella. "Start bringing the outliers into the castle and tell the farmers and villagers to be alert. Any traveler or person on the road or crossing fields must be treated with suspicion and intolerance and brought to the castle before they may continue on their journey after they have been searched for weapons."

When the stretcher was taken down to the kitchen and Callum laid on one of the scrubbed tables, Ella saw Oswald sitting on a little stool next to the open fire pit. "Oswald! How nice to see you again." She saw the young lad open his mouth to ask questions, so Ella cut him off. "Run to the steward and tell him to make a list of supplies inside the castle walls." Suddenly she remembered. "The castle walls - are they finished yet?"

One of the servants helping the rowers lay Callum onto the table on his side and volunteered the information. "It is some few yards short o' completion, lady."

Ella stared at the men in amazement. "Well, whatever are you waiting for? Go forth and finish it now!"

The men bustled out, leaving Ella alone with the kitchen maids and the Cook. "Who works in the scullery?" Ella wanted to know. Three maids put up their hands. "You are to be in charge of boiling the water. Don't touch the table." The scullery was always the least hygienic part of a kitchen as it dealt with food scraps and wastewater.

"The page boy has gone to fetch the pincers, Milady," the Cook told Ella. "Good," Ella was too focused on what must be done to be polite. "Now, go and wash your hands. You are to help me keep Callum on his side. Can you do that?"

After many years of having access to food, the Cook was more than capable of heaving Callum sideways with her shoulders. She kept him there by gripping his wrists and elbow. "We do his back first and then the chest." The page boy ran into the kitchen with a pair of large metal pliers. "Oor blacksmith took these straight oot o' the fire, lady!" he said to Ella.

She had unfolded a disposable dressing sheet onto the table and snapped on some gloves, much to the fascination of the boy helping her. Ella sprayed the pincer edges with antiseptic and then did the same to the bolt tip sticking out of Callum's thick back muscle; she did not want to withdraw the bolt from his chest and drag germs all the way through his body while she did it.

Quieting her nerves, Ella brought up the plier edges to the bolt's tip and cut off the barb. It was a good enough job even though the pressure made the bolt wobble inside the flesh, but the wood shaft splintered slightly. Leaning closer, she checked which way the splinters were angled, not wanting to drag minute shards of wood into Callum's body.

I can't wait. I must complete the operation before Callum starts rising to consciousness again. Spraying the exit site with antiseptic and then laying Callum down on a clean gauze dressing, moving to stand next to the Cook at a slight angle so that the withdrawing motion was at the same degree as the quarrel bolt, Ella wrapped her hands around the fletch.

"Lady, let me help ye," Cook insisted. "The flesh grips the barb with a strength that will surprise ye."

Standing side by side, the two women grasped the bolt fletch and pulled with all their might. Cook had been right; the quarrel was deeply embedded in the body, already melded to the flesh and bone in a very disturbing way. They heaved and gasped, and the bolt slid out inch by inch until the chest muscle yielded the shaft with a hideous grating sound as it left the shoulder blade bone.

After changing her gloves because her hands had touched the bolt, Ella asked Cook to turn Callum onto his side again. The exit wound was bleeding freely now that nothing was blocking the hole. Grimacing but steady, Ella inserted her finger into the hole to check for venal hemorrhaging before stuffing the wound full of antibiotics and cocaine to stop the bleeding. After twisting the cap off a fresh tube of super glue and dotting it onto the ragged flaps of skin and muscle, she sealed the wound shut by pinching the site closed with her fingers. She did the same with the wound on the right side of his chest under the collarbone after Cook had laid Callum's back down on the table.

Ella had learned the finest makeshift emergency battlefield dressing techniques the twenty-first century could offer - all she'd had to do was bring the strange medicines in her backpack. She remembered how heavy the pack had been as she ran through the museum toward the charmstone, but it had all been worth it.

With a dose of cocaine leaching into his system from the wound sites, it was only a matter of time before Callum woke up. Ella had asked one of the porters at the hotel in Edinburgh to hook her up with the best drug dealer in town; she was sure that the cocaine was premium quality, potent enough to constrict any blood vessel it came into contact with.

While she dressed and bandaged Callum's right shoulder and arm, he began stirring, uttering harsh grunts of pain and confusion. Quietly asking Cook to send for the men with the stretcher, Ella wrapped her arms around Callum's legs and began weeping, something she had wanted to do from the first time she saw that evil looking quarrel bolt sticking out of his chest.

Chapter Twelve

"She's a healer, no' a witch!" Oswald insisted on telling one of the scullery maids. "Ella is a good, kind lady!"

The scullion sniffed. "Och, awa' wi' ye, Ozzy. The clouds have hung heavy in the skies since the wummin arrived here. Maybe she has other items o' witchcraft in that magician's bag of hers. A storm in a jar? A man's heart pierced with a thorn or a womb full of lunar pain?"

"Is nae oor Cal still alive?" Oswald wanted to make his point.

"Aye, alive and enslaved by her unnatural charms an' moon silver hair!" One of the scullions joined in the conversation. "And she acts so unnatural since making Kilchurn her home, what with her banshee wailin' over the master's fever an' gatherin' the men for meetings in the master's bedchamber."

This much was true. At first, Ella had been stricken with regret and despair about Callum's injury. She did not leave his side for three days, thinking nothing when she had to use the pot in the corner as a toilet or run affairs while leaning against the bolster at the head of the bed.

If she wanted a change of scenery, she would look out of the narrow bedchamber windows. The left side window overlooked the herb garden, such as it was; half a dozen ale barrels sawn in twain and planted with pale sage, purple lavender, dill, fennel, parsley, and thyme and placed carefully against the warm castle stone wall to guard them against inclement weather. Sometimes while she watched, Ella would see the sluice gate drain eject water, and she would stand and gaze as the damp stain turned the stones in the wall black as it dripped down.

The right window had a view of the outer perimeter wall. Already, it was being used to house poultry. Geese and hens picked over the vegetable peelings, strutting around the wisps of hay on the ground and hissing whenever a goat came too close. The wall was almost complete and fortifications were already being made for the stables.

The moment she had known Callum was stable and as comfortable as the twenty-first century medicines she had brought with her could make him, Ella sprang into action, righteous anger burning inside her stomach.

"Andrew and Eamon Campbell? You remember me, do you not?"

She summoned two of Callum's soldiers to the bedchamber, describing them to the page boy so he could fetch the men to her."

"Aye, Lady. We are clan, and Cal is oor captain. We were there the day he rescued ye from the brigands."

Ella bowed her head in acknowledgment. "For which I am grateful to you both every day. But that's not why I ask you to come here - much water has flown under the bridge since we first met. Sir Col has recognized Callum as his rightful son and heir. Laird Stewart has sworn an oath to say that Lady Mariot birthed Callum while Black Colin was on crusade. The Lady of Loch Awe gave him over to Laird Gerwain, who duly gave Callum back to his father for fostering until he judged it was the right time to tell them - that time was lately."

Andrew whistled. "Woo! If there was bad blood between Duncan an' Cal after ye came along, 'twill be naught compared to what the man must be feelin' after hearin' aboot that."

Ella agreed. "Indeed. With all the back and forth-," Ella did not want to go into too much detail about what had happened after Laird Gerwain revealed the truth "-word about Duncan's displacement must have leaked out to Lady Margaret's camp. I want you to sally forth and find someone who can place Duncan, or any of Lady Margaret's followers, at the riverbanks today. Leave some men to help finish the wall, but the rest must help you scour the countryside. I want the bowman caught - and I want him alive."

It was as if Ella had grown up overnight. The attack on Callum was the catalyst she needed to jump from awkwardly modern teen to calculating medieval mistress. She could feel her wrath boiling with every breath she took, but after everything that had happened to her, Ella now had the discipline to act slowly and deliberately. Callum could not search for his would-be assassin, so she must do it for him.

Eamon suggested they ride to the village to pick up any rumors about which way the wind was blowing over at Lady Margaret's manor house before going from farmstead to cottage to ask about who might have been seen on the roads.

As they left, Ella was reminded to say, "The rogue struck as we rowed past Innis Chonain shoals, so he has great knowledge about the boat routes. Start your search on that side of the loch, at the bothy at the foot of the mountain."

"Cruachan?" Eamon suggested. Ella shrugged. "I have not lived here long enough to know, but it is the bothy by the river shoals."

Ella lay back against the bolster, staring at the overhead canopy of the four-poster bed. This was where she and Callum had first made love. This is where Ella had experienced the most exquisite sensations of pleasure and pain, where she had sighed and softly moaned in equal measure in between passionate bouts of kissing. This is where she had grown to understand the fine art of arousal and affection.

Turning onto her side, she watched the Highlander's motionless eyelids. The dark lashes did not flicker or blink to show he was dreaming or asleep: Callum was unconscious. Ella swallowed her panic, focusing on the emergency medical training course she had attended.

"If a main vein has been hit, the blood will be dark. You will need to dig into the wound, locate the injured vessel, and use the super glue to seal it. Likewise, if the blood is red, you know it's an artery - an oxygen-carrying vessel. Super glue the site, add a vasoconstrictor such as cocaine or ephedrine to the wound, and then super glue it shut. If the injury is a flesh wound, the same technique applies but without the vessel sealing. If you have access to antibiotics, administer them. If not, use raw honey."

She had done exactly what the instructor had said, but Callum remained pale, still, and silent - and while that was good as far as healing was concerned, but bad for Ella's peace of mind. Had she overdosed him with painkillers? Had she missed a severed blood vessel? Would he ever come out of what was rapidly starting to look like a coma? Her nights were interrupted by fear that he had died in his sleep. Ella would wake up sweating, only to place her ear against the left side of Callum's chest to check that he was still breathing, before moistening the inside of his mouth and lips with boiled water.

Tears would run down Ella's face as she stared at her lover. Callum was so much more to her than someone who could make her feel as if she was transported to heaven whenever she lay in his arms - he was her soul mate and best friend. Only three years ago, she had been an isolated teenager attending high school in an obscure town in a remote part of the world, and now she was…but the word 'now' did not mean anything to Ella anymore. She had never been obscure or remote: all she had ever been was a woman destined to travel back in time to join herself to the person destined to carry the other half of the Campbell charmstone.

Giving a hysterical laugh, Ella threw herself back on the bed and gave herself over to complete misery. Without Callum, she was alone in an alien place and time. It only reaffirmed her sorrow when her loud screams of sadness did not rouse Callum from his deep slumber.

As the days passed, the Castle Kilchurn servants got into the habit of visiting Ella to give her news and receive tasks. Thus it was that she grew to learn about what was happening outside the four walls of Callum's bedchamber. Sir Colin and Laird Gerwain had joined forces and assembled their soldiers in preparation for battle. River Awe was patrolled all along the banks; Eamon and Andrew had discovered the footprints where the bowman had concealed himself and had been able to track them north and east as far as Glenorchy parish.

"Father Archibald," Ella said in a dull voice. It had been over five days since the attack, and Callum had not fully woken. He would take water when she lifted his head and hold a cup to his mouth but then sink back down soon after.

Ella had allowed the healer to help her change the soiled sheets and scatter fragrant herbs into the water she used to bathe him, but that was the only medieval medicine Ella permitted near her beloved patient.

"Might we put out a reward?" Andrew suggested. "Might that not be the best way to find witnesses?"

Ella shook her head. "Nay. We cannot match any offer the Bishop of Rutherglen will have made, and a reward for information will bring forth those who want to trade lies for gold. Keep looking."

Other pieces of news trickled in: Lady Margaret had sent Duncan to the King to beseech the monarch to intervene on his behalf, and the manor house occupants had found the cellar escape tunnel and blocked it off. The Bishop had sent twenty soldiers to guard the manor, but other than that, he seemed to have distanced himself from the Lady's enterprise.

Ella spent the rest of the day chatting to Callum about the craziness of her previous life: chuckling about how far removed people had grown from food production, making thoughtful observations about the dilemma between the sacredness of human life and the futility of urban overpopulation; she told him how the divide between rich and poor had only increased over the centuries, and what the Enlightenment had done to bring about the ascendance of science.

"Nothing much has changed socially during my time, my dearest love," Ella concluded, "except now we can harness electricity to power our machines."

Callum shifted, which made the bed creak. He opened his eyes. "Ella," he managed to croak out the word.

Everything in her life fell back into place. Moving closer to her dear patient, Ella said, "Oh, Callum. You're alive. I've been so worried." Ella's throat was too tight for her to continue speaking. Callum tried to laugh but winced before the sound came out of his mouth, changing it to a groan of pain.

"Och, lass," Callum's mouth was so dry, his voice was rough, "what malady struck me doon?"

"Hush, love," she said, cradling his head under her arm so he could lift it up and drink from the cup she was holding to his mouth. "You must heal some more before you worry your mind over that."

"Are ye safe?" he asked after swallowing some water.

"I am now," Ella assured him.

Chapter Thirteen

That evening, Andrew and Eamon returned to bring news to the bed-chamber and found their captain sitting up in bed, spooning gruel into his mouth by using his left hand. He was still pale and the pain he must be feeling was etched clearly on his face, but other than the more obvious signs of invalidism, he was the same Captain Callum Campbell.

"I suppose ye'll be wantin' us to call ye 'Sir Knight' noo?" Eamon offered up by way of greeting.

"Is this yer idea of grabbing a couple o' days off work?" Andrew asked gruffly.

"Awa' wit' both o' ye an' go bile yer heids." Callum countered.

With these greetings out of the way, the three men fell to talking. No one bothered mentioning the fine job that Ella had done running things during Callum's illness because it was clear to everyone that she had acted in a sensible manner from the time he had fallen back in the boat with a bolt sticking out of his chest. They would waste no time in heaping praise on her. Always practical, the Highlanders believed that if Ella did not have the good sense to admire herself for her heroic actions, there was no use in them trying to do it for her!

"We have good news an' it's waitin' outside. One of oor own clan has returned from Glenorchy with a tale to tell. What say ye to us in-vitin' the fellow in so that we might judge him honest?" Andrew said. After Callum nodded, Eamon went to the door and opened it. A farmer whom Callum recognized entered.

"Greetings, Sir Cal," the man began, but Callum waved his left hand in a dismissive gesture. "I have nae been formally acknowledged as a Knight o' the realm yet, Master David. Call me captain 'til such a time as me title is more widely kent."

The farmer bowed and then continued. "I journeyed to the market five days ago, takin' the boat across to Dalmally along the south banks, plannin' to continue on foot to Glenorchy. While fastenin' me boat after reachin' the south banks of the River Orchy, I spied yer…half-brither, Duncan, trampin' through the reeds. He had a crossbow slung behind his back and a pallet tied around his shoulders. When I greeted him, he showed himself reluctant to name me but did so by an' by. I asked him if he had lost a horse - that lonely area of lush grassland being a favorite place for runaway mounts to wander through on their way back to Kilchurn stables - but he disavowed it entirely, saying he was traveling to be shriven at Glenorchy. I made a jest, saying that the dealings at the manor house must be lewd for the young gentleman to be hastening on foot to give Father Archibald his confession, but he grew silent and told me to be gone."

Ella believed the farmer was telling the truth, and when she looked at Callum she could see he was of the same mind.

"I thank ye most graciously for bringin' us this news, Master. This rings true more than ye ken. Duncan must have told Lady Margaret about bumpin' into ye, an' so they sent him off to the King to make out that oor Duncan was there all along." Callum said calmly. He placed the spoon back into the bowl slowly, still getting used to doing everything with his left hand. "One question. Did it look as if Duncan had been sleeping roughly? Could it have been that his horse lost a shoe, and he was forced to complete the journey on foot?"

The farmer gave the question some thought before replying. "The first one. The pallet was soiled with riverbank debris: damp grass and mud marks. Surely he would have made the trip by boat or chosen to billet somewhere drier if he had lost his mount?"

Eamon showed the farmer out, leaving the other three to comment freely on the update.

"It was Duncan! Duncan tried to murder you!" Ella was almost incandescent with rage. She jumped off the bed and nearly fell off the dais, so eager was she to confront Duncan. "Eamon, Andrew! Make ready the horses and gather the soldiers - we leave for that midden muck manor house anon!"

But the two soldiers did not move. They stood firm, waiting for Callum's order which came soon enough. "Ella! This is a chess game, no' a match o' spillikins. Sit doon."

She couldn't sit down but went to stand next to Callum's side of the bed, ready to interject her opinion into the discussion. In her eyes, he still looked weak and ever so slightly anemic. There were mauve stains under his eyes and a drawn look to his angular cheekbones under the red beard scruff. She could not even begin to imagine what the upper right side of his chest must feel like.

When his beloved blue eyes flickered open and stared up at her for the first time after the attack, Ella had been overjoyed. She had administered one of her precious multivitamin fizzing tablets to him as soon as he had drunk some barley water and kept it down. Within hours, Callum had been sitting up and demanding to know what had happened to him on the River Awe boat ride.

He seemed remarkably sanguine after hearing about the attempt to take his life: looking at him now, Ella had to think Callum suspected something like this would happen sooner or later.

"Bishop Rutherglen has passed the fight over to Duncan if I am to be any judge o' the matter." Callum spoke deliberately, thinking and plotting at the same time. "Let's no' add another front to guard by involvin' him any longer. The Bishop's nephew, Glynnis, is betrothed to Laird Gerwain Stewart's heiress, young Margaret. The Bishop would never wager against the Rutherglen family gaining such a rich connection. However, let oor enemies *think* that's where we are focusin' oor energies."

The subalterns had to come closer to hear what Callum was saying, because his speech was low and strained. Ella went to pour another mug of barley water, but Callum refused it with a short shake of his head when she held it out to him.

Instead of being put out by this sign of impatience, Ella was encouraged, seeing it as proof that Callum was slowly becoming his old self.

"The Bishop would have sent soldiers to the manor house under the guise of protection, but the men will take their orders from Father Archibald."

"It is unheard of that a cleric act in a war-like fashion against his liege laird!" Andrew shook his head in disbelief. "Whether he uses the soldiers to attack or defend, it is treasonous."

"Duncan must have sold him a yarn aboot the priest owin' his allegiance," Callum said in an even tone. "If I were lyin' dead with a crossbow bolt through me eye, would it no' be true? Besides, auld

Archibald kent his goose was well an' truly cooked from the time he relished the thought of torturin' me wummin."

Eamon's brow furrowed. "What if the rascal sends his soldiers forth? He's done it before under the guise of witch hunting - he could do it again."

Callum shook his head. "He played that tune before, and it failed; he will nae try it again. Nor will he send soldiers forth from the manor house, no' with the Bishop's ordering the priest and Lady Margaret to play the victim. Nay, they will wait for us to go to them, so they will have cause to supplicate to the King or the Pope."

"The King's on oor side," Andrew said, "he got that wee parcel o' fancy jewels ye sent him."

It made sense. If Callum ordered anyone to seek out Duncan, only then would Father Archibald have an excuse to sally forth from the manor house. If the occupants of Kilchurn Castle continued as normal, so would those living at the manor be forced to do so.

A deadlock.

"B-but what about vengeance?" Ella was aghast. She wanted to see Duncan grovel, that creepy, overdressed, sneaky molester!

Callum shot her a smile, with Eamon and Andrew even laughing. "It's hard waiting for the hammer to fall, Lady." Andrew chuckled. "Especially such a hammer as the Captain wields."

It sounded as if Callum was getting stronger every time he spoke. "In the meantime, we will make the hammer in a more crafty fashion."

***

A fortnight later, Callum and Ella were lying in bed together, doing something they had come to enjoy - holding their charmstones aloft and staring at the crystals.

It was something Callum liked to do with his right hand, seeing how long he could hold his arm in the air before the pain forced him to lower it. Ella found pleasure from the way her crystal shot the occasional spark of light out of its opaque body. When they did this together, she noticed that Callum's charmstone would emit a tiny burst of light at the same time, as if the two halves were secretly communicating their harmony to one another.

"What shall we do with them once this imbroglio is over?" Callum asked Ella as he lifted his right arm up and down, bending and flexing it while biting back the discomfort.

Thinking he was talking about Duncan, Lady Margaret, and Father Archibald, Ella shook her head, mussing her silver-blonde hair on the bolster as she did so. "I don't envy you, Callum. As a Knight of the Realm, your jurisprudence in the matter will define you for the rest of your rule. Still, I have a suspicion that medieval justice for such treachery and an attempted assassination might be severe."

"Hangin', drawin', and quarterin' for the men; hangin' or beheadin' for the wummin - they rose up against their laird, who is himself an extension o' the King." Callum saw Ella wince and sucked air through his teeth, lowering the charmstone until it lay on his chest. "But I was talking about the talismans, sweetheart. I dinnae want to keep the poor wee things, no' when they might take it into their minds to spirit ye awa' from me at any moment."

That made Ella laugh and forget her worries. "The charmstones can hardly have minds of their own, Callum! They are rocks."

He shook his head. "I think those practitioners of magick stumbled upon something beyond their comprehension an' harnessed it to the best o' their knowledge. Those mages are fanatics. I ken a zealot when I see one. They dinnae understand the true intent and purpose o' the magick of the stones."

The more Ella thought about it, the less she liked the idea of her family having access to a charmstone that might throw them into the past willy-nilly, but nor did she want to lose the crystal. Callum shifted closer to her, turning onto his left side so they might look at one another face to face.

"Ella, ye saved me life an' ye *are* me life. I swear a true love vow to ye forever. Would the healers from yer era allow us to join oor bodies at this time, d'ye think?"

She was thrilled by his tentative query and gladly agreed to them trying. They were lying in bed in their nightshirts with the summer sun warming the cold castle stone walls outside; the air smelt of the lavender and mint Ella had picked out of the kitchen garden and placed in a mug by the bedside. What better way to greet the day than by doing what Callum had suggested?

But the rollicking activity that Callum attempted proved to be too sore for him to sustain. After gingerly biting her thumbnail with embarrassment, Ella said, "They already call me a witch down in the kitchens, so I have nothing to lose. There is something from my time that we could try…"

"Well then," Callum's face lit up at the prospect, "why are ye still lyin' there, lass? Tell me what it is!"

Blushing so deeply that Ella thought her cheeks must light up the bedchamber, she dared to continue. "Well, the lady takes the lead, taking the man's position on top," only by covering her face with two hands was Ella able to continue, "-and so doing all the work for him."

"It sounds unnatural," Callum frowned, "I have nae even seen such an act drawn in the margins of the prayer books before."

Emboldened, Ella said, "Yes, I know all about those rude little drawings made on the sides of medieval books, but prayer book marginalia doodles were all drawn by men! Of course, they will focus on bending a lady over or covering her in the bed."

"Ha!" Callum looked pleased, "you're no' so shy when it comes to defendin' yer suggestion, are ye, Ella? ye wee minx!"

Their experimentation was a resounding success, and Callum encouraged Ella to take the lead for the rest of his convalescence. They were in no hurry to leave the bedchamber, and when Callum eventually came downstairs to check on the wall defenses a good couple of months after the attempt on his life, Andrew took one look at him and said with a wink. "Ye're lookin' better noo than ye did afore the ambush, Cal. Would we all lay a-bed with oor ladies for a month or two."

"Andrew, lad," Callum returned the wink, "ye have nay idea how right ye are."

Chapter Fourteen

"The time for aggressive forays has passed." Black Colin had returned to join his son in debate. "Ye have two choices: attack the manor with full force, or sneak inside at night an' take the key players captive."

"They've been skulkin' in that bloody manor hoose for weeks; they are hardly likely to venture forth since that scoundrel, Duncan, came back from Sterling with his news." Andrew grumbled.

As the eldest, he had been made captain of the guards since the decree recognizing Callum as a Knight of the Realm had arrived. All of Duncan's plotting and pleading with the King had come to naught once Laird Gerwain Stewart had produced documents of proof regarding Callum's origins and parentage., and once Duncan had been stripped of his title as Sir Colin Campbell's heir, he no longer had any standing at court. Thus he was forced to travel back to the manor house, this time without his merry retinue of followers or wearing gay attire tailor made to fit his slender form.

"What say ye, Cal?" Eamon cocked an eye at the new Knight of Kilchurn Castle. "Stealth or head-on?"

"Stealth." Callum swung his new sword above his head and then around his body in mesmerizing circles. "Me faither an' I will do it."

The four men were standing inside the outer perimeter walls of the castle, ostensibly to inspect the building works but really to plot. "We'll set forth tonight," Callum spoke as lightly as if he were planning a trip to the market. "Duncan is to be taken alive - he is me faither's son after all - but Lady Margaret and the priest are worm meat."

Andrew noticed that Callum had not referred to Duncan as 'half-brother,' and yet it was that thin blood connection that would save Duncan Campbell's life, or at least postpone his death. The man was to be taken alive and sent to Sterling to await judgment.

Just before the party broke up, Callum reminded them. "Dinnae say a word to Milady. She is no' used to oor ways."

"Ye don' have to say that twice," Eamon growled under his breath. "Frankly, I'm amazed she let ye ootside without a nanny to hold yer hand, lad."

Callum chuckled. "Och aye, the lass is thrawn, but all she does 'tis done with a good heart. When all this is finished, I will wed her."

Such romantic chit-chat was too flowery for the men. The small group broke up and went their separate ways: Black Colin to hone his sword blade, Callum to tell the grooms to feed and water two black ponies. The soldiers to oversee bow practice at the village - Callum had ordered two dozen crossbows to be made, and they wanted to teach the male villagers how to use them.

This was all for the benefit of anyone watching the castle from the vantage point of the hill. Callum knew that the sentry sent to spy on them would return to the manor house in time for his supper and tell its occupants that Sir Callum's army showed no sign of aggression.

He could see them all now. Duncan would scratch his head, no expert in retaliation tactics, and tell his mother that he had known all along that Callum Campbell was a poltroon and a coward. Father Archibald would smile smugly, bless the company with one wave of his fat hand, and conclude that the church's grace kept him safe from vengeful acts.

The image made Callum smile grimly.

"What's so amusing?" Ella asked him. Whenever he looked at her, Callum felt his heart leap with joy. The woman had fallen into his life like an angel from heaven, and just as beautiful as one too. Castle life suited Ella. Her face had lost its drawn appearance, growing soft and round, as had her wrists and arms. Her skin glowed, and so did her eyes wherever she glanced at him. She had worn her hair under a hood, even though the benefit of marriage had not been bestowed on her yet, because Ella knew he liked her to do so. Now her silver hair was for his eyes alone.

"Naught," Callum replied. "I smile because I am happy."

She muttered something about it being a serious smile and not a happy one, but Ella allowed it to pass.

It wrenched his heart to leave her that night. Placing the charm-stone next to her head on the pillow, Callum crept outside to dress in the stairwell. It was here that Black Colin found him.

"Be swift," he said softly, shooting a glance at the thick bed-chamber door as he checked for sounds of movement behind it.

"Hang aboot, auld man," Callum whispered as he tightened the belt around his plaid and stood up, "these things take time."

"Bar the entrance and hold it fast 'til we return," Callum told the sentries at the entrance. The ponies were waiting for them at the bottom of the stone steps.

A few moments later, the two men had set the ponies trotting over the rough heather tufted hills. They were not using the beaten trail but cutting across the wilds. Their boots stopped the thistles and brambles from pricking their legs, but it was hard going all the same. The waxing crescent moon gave no light, but both men knew the hills surrounding the castle like the back of their hands.

They knew where to tether the ponies so any sound of grass being chewed would not reach the sentries on duty and they knew at what angle to approach the manor walls and where to scale them.

It was all done in silence; father and son used hand signals when they needed to communicate. Callum had the idea to enter through the roof door where he had seen Ella standing after she got lost in the labyrinth of passages.

By prearrangement, Callum and Colin went in different directions once they were inside and had opened the window shutters ajar to give them some light: Callum headed to Father Archibald's chambers, where the guests were housed. The business was completed ruthlessly, and the priest was dispatched with no noise. Wiping his dirk on the bed covers, Callum went to rendezvous with his father outside Duncan's rooms.

He was not kept waiting. Black Colin padded down the passage toward him, only discernible from the faint sound of his breathing. Nodding to his son, the old knight unhooked the small bundle of kindling he had brought with him. Kneeling down to place it by Duncan's door and scraping his tinder flint over it, the bundle of twigs began to burn, small flames at first, but they soon found the dry timber door and licked at it greedily.

Smoke filled the passage, but still, the two men waited. Even if Duncan had gone to bed dead drunk, one of his lackeys would alert him. The sound of the door bar lifting could be heard above the crackle of the fire. Four men burst out of the doorway, coughing and clamoring. Colin and Callum cut three of them down when they saw they were not Duncan. The fourth man was spared long enough to answer a question.

"Where's yer master?"

"The moon is dark tonight - he said he was going to the castle-,"

Duncan was more like his father than they suspected. He was using the cover of the waning crescent moon to try and find a way into Kilchurn Castle.

Leaving the fire to burn, Callum and Black Colin ran out into the courtyard. The gates were open to allow the servants to flee. Cries of 'fire!' could be heard as smoke began to pour out of the windows. As Callum sped toward the ponies, he looked over his shoulder and saw the flames licking the manor rooftop.

A vision of Ella standing on the rooftop, her kirtle so short that he could see the hem flapping around her slim ankles, and as he hailed her, she had turned and looked down at him with a smile that lit up his heart with many emotions. Yes, even then, he had known she was his soul's desire.

There was no need for secrecy any longer. Callum spurred the pony with his heels, urging the sturdy beast into a gallop. It seemed like an age, but it was not much later that they reached the castle.

Dismounting with stealth and leaving the animal to graze unattended, Callum crept back up the stone steps and scratched on the door. One of the sentries opened. "Two o' ye - come with me."

They marched around the castle with their necks craned to look up at the tall walls. The crescent moon was hidden behind thick clouds; it was black as pitch outside, with no moonlight to guide them. One of the guards stumbled on the rocks, biting back a curse.

The other guard tugged at Callum's shirt sleeve, pointing at the kitchen sluice hole. Camouflaged by the dark water stain on the stone was a rope. It hung down from one of the kitchen windows that had been left open. Callum debated which way would be faster: to go back around to the front entrance or climb up the rope. He chose the rope. The guards wove their hands together so they could lift him up. Using this as a step, Callum began climbing. After reaching the window, Callum saw it would be a tight fit for him. His shoulders were twice as broad as Duncan's, but he pushed inside, tearing his shirt in the process. It was painful for his shoulder and chest to hold his weight, but not intolerable. Finding a grappling hook embedded inside the kitchen wall, Callum was pleased to know Duncan had no help from those inside the castle.

Like a deadly, dark shadow, Callum treaded deliberately up the stairs, balancing his back against the wall to feel out the steps with his feet first. It was a long way up to the turret, but Callum did not make a misstep; his focus was as keen as his blade.

Callum found the bedchamber door ajar, which was not how he had left it. From the sounds coming from the bed, he knew Duncan had not been able to resist having a dalliance with Ella before taking her captive. The knave! He would have been able to place himself in a far better position if he had made off with Ella back out of the window and down the rope after rendering her unconscious, but no. He had forfeited that just for the chance to ravage a sleeping woman.

The time for caution had passed, because Ella's charmstone might speed her away at any moment, as repulsed by Duncan's act as she was herself.

Entering the room, Callum heard the muffled screams and frantic kicking get louder. He could discern no words, but knew there was a fierce struggle happening on the bed. Callum had never bothered finding out if Duncan preferred his females to be meek or fiery, but he suspected it was the latter. Even if the man failed in escaping and taking Ella with him, Duncan would cherish this event for the rest of his life - if he had managed to achieve it.

The struggling and muffled gasps stopped as Callum placed the sharp point of his dirk at the back of his half-brother's neck, saying, "Move a finger, an' ye're dead." Immediately, Duncan flopped like a rag doll, collapsing on Ella's neck as if he wanted to hide his face with shame.

A relieved sob let him know that Ella was whole.

"Push him off ye, sweetheart, and slide out from underneath him," Callum told Ella in a calm voice. She obeyed him, pulling her nightgown down and climbing off the dais. She went to stand in the corner, as far away from Duncan as possible. "Go unshutter the window and lift the drape."

She did as he bid her, but Ella returned to stand in the corner.

"Did he penetrate ye?" Callum did not look at Ella; all of his concentration was on the back of Duncan's neck.

"No," Ella's voice rasped, telling Callum with no words that Duncan had throttled her to keep her quiet. Black Colin stepped into the room; he must have ridden his pony like the wind to reach the castle in Callum's wake.

The old man sighed as he took in the tableau presented by the faint outline of moonlight. "Och, Duncan. Ye could have been a wise and just man, but ye took the other road, lad."

In a business-like way, Colin stepped over to the bed. Grabbing Duncan by the hair, he pulled the man's head back to expose his throat. Ella gasped from the corner of the room as Black Colin withdrew a dirk from his belt, but the elderly man scoffed. "Dinnae fash, girl. I'm only doin' this," and with those words, Colin poked the knife into Duncan's ear canal. "Can ye feel that? Blink if ye do, 'cause if ye nod, the point will drive into yer brain box."

Duncan must have blinked. "Good," Colin said, "noo turn 'round slowly an' step doon the dais."

By the time Duncan stumbled to the floor, Callum had lit a candle. Using his knife to lift up the hem of Duncan's plaid, Callum bent down and used the candlelight to inspect Duncan's privates. "Just in case Milady's soft heart caused her to lie aboot yer incursion, crow meat," Callum told Duncan in a cheerful voice. Then he nodded to his father, who marched out of the door with his dirk still lightly embedded in Duncan's ear.

After darting a look at Ella in her corner, he said. "I'll be back anon. I must light the fellow downstairs so that he does nae fall and break his own neck to cheat the hangman."

Taking the candle with him, Callum left Ella alone in the dark.

***

It took longer for Ella to regain her serenity than it had for Callum to regain the full use of his shoulder. As deeply as the crossbow quarrel bolt had penetrated his chest, so had Duncan been able to strip away Ella's peace of mind.

Ever since the night of the fire, Ella had lain in bed, listless and weak, as if the attack had been conducted by a vampire whose mission it was to suck the life force out of her.

When Callum approached her with affection or desire, she would turn away from him with a sigh and a shrug. Being young and inexperienced when it came to the ways of women, Callum spent more time training his men or riding the boundaries of his demesne, chatting to the farmers and villagers.

"Is she eatin'?" his father asked him one evening. The two men were seated in the side chamber where the portrait of Mariot, the Lady of Loch Awe smiled mistily down at them.

"Well enough," Callum said, "but she pines for something I cannot give her, though I don' ken what it is."

Colin was a canny man. "She'll be bonny again after ye tell her aboot young Margaret's marriage. Ask her if she wants the next vows to be between the two o' ye. Remind her that she is yer peerless paramour an' ye cannae live without her."

After scoffing at his father's attempt at prose, Callum wasted no time in running up to the turret. He found Ella out of bed, but still in her nightgown. She was reading a book in the sunlight beaming through the window, and made such a pretty picture that she nearly took his breath away.

"Sweetheart, do ye go well? What book are ye readin'?"

With a deep sigh, Ella showed Callum the book: The Breadalbane Muniments associated with the Black Book of Taymouth: Their Relation to Highland Heroes, Myths, & Legends.

Kneeling at her side, Callum held one of Ella's hands. "I came here to tell ye that young Margaret is wed. She belongs to Glynnis noo," Callum paused a beat before continuing, "just as I wish for ye to belong to me, Ella, for I would never want to wake an' see another lady lyin' next to me. Ye are me Lady of Loch Awe."

It was a clumsy proposal, but it was the best he could do - Callum had never been the sort of man to think hard before saying something because he was a naturally thoughtful man speaking straight from the heart.

Placing her book down carefully on her lap, Ella said, "Who told you?"

This strange reply did not take Callum by surprise. "I deemed it right to resume diplomatic relations with Rutherglen. I strongly suspect the Bishop's nephew, Glynnis, and young Margaret might be your ancestors. If so, it would not be a betrayal for us to hand yer charmstone over to them when the time is right."

Ella smiled. It was the first time he had seen her smile since the attack, and Callum's heart soared when he saw it, only to crash down again when she shook her head.

But it was not to say no. "So, you don't know."

The world and its place on the Great Spiral seemed to stand still for Callum and Ella as he asked the question. "Know what?"

"It was bound to happen sooner and not later, Callum," Ella smiled. "I am with child. I don't know anything about pregnancy, but I think it must have happened after the crossbow attack. That's why I've been so…different. I wanted to ensure the night's shock had not harmed the child sleeping inside me."

He did not overreact. Callum was too disciplined to shout and caper at the thought of their union bringing forth new life. The sound of the men returning from harvesting the fields could be heard through the window. Their wives and children went out to offer them ale. The leaves were turning on the tree boughs, and soon they would fall.

Placing his hand and then his head on Ella's softly rounded belly, the two of them stayed like that for a long time.

Neither Callum nor Ella would have been surprised to know that the moment was watched and approved of by Khronos, Aion, and Kairos, because, after all they had been through, what really was time and space anyway, when compared to love?

THE END

The Mysteries Of Mull Series
Book 1. The Highlander And The Enchanting Lass
Book 2. The Captain And His Scottish Lassie
Book 3. Healing Her Highlander Before Christmas
Book 4. The Highlander's Hostage Bride
The Mysteries Of Mull Series Complete Series
(All four books in one)

The Masters Of Overtoun Bridge Series
Book 1. The Bridge Through Time
Book 2. The Thrill Of The Chase
Book 3. Third Time's The Charm
The Masters Of Overtoun Bridge Complete Series
(All three books in one)

Conall Clyde/Wolf River Series
Book 1. Wolf's Battle
Book 2. Wolf's Enslavement
Book 3 Wolf's Revenge
The Conall Clyde -Wolf River Complete Series
(All three books in one)

The Lady Of Loch Awe Series
Book 1. Enchanted BY The Highlander
Book 2. Making Magic With The Highlander
Book 3. Destined To Be With The Highlander
The Lady Of Loch Awe Complete Series
(All three books in one)

Love At Bamburgh Castle Series
Book 1. "Say I Do" At Bamburgh Castle
Book 2. Christmas At Bamburgh Castle
Book 3. The Highland Chieftain's Heart

Love At Bamburgh Castle Complete Series
(All three books in one)

The Seath Mor Series
Book 1. The Bride's Black Mirror
Book 2. The Lady's Black Quill
Book 3. The Highland Thane's Warrior Wife
The Seath Mor Sgorfhiaclach Complete Series
(All three books in one)

Look for Kalani's books on

www.kmbookstore.com